# The Curtain Twitchers of Oakley Place

Deborah Hodgetts

# DEDICATION

To all Seekers of the Truth

# Foreword

*What once was a dream*
*has now come to pass,*
*as stone and the clay*
*were first ether and gas.*

*In the game of life*
*your dreams will come alive,*
*by thinking of the end result*
*as if it had arrived*

*Time and space*
*aren't as they seem . . .*
*just magical props*
*in a magical dream.*

*Believe in yourself*
*and soon you will see,*
*how happy and free*
*you were meant to be.*

*lessed are emotions,*
*for though some make you weep,*
*you're better to have known them*
*for the secrets that they keep.*

*Life's an illusion*
*just waiting for you . . .*
*to act on your dreams*
*so that they can come true.*

©Mike Dooley, www.tut.com

*Taken from 'An Adventurer's Guide to the Jungles of time and Space' by*
*Mike Dooley.*

# Chapter One
# The Beginning

In this quaint idyllic village lurked the watchers, perched in their places of safety looking out into the bleakness of the day. Their eyes pierced the depths of my soul, clawing and drawing my safety from within.

I had just moved to this leafy village in the depths of the Buckinghamshire countryside, from the chaos of the big smoke. I thought I had escaped those Curtain Twitchers; those beings of solitude entrapped and entrapping like thieves of your sanity.

To the visitors who were just passing through this village, everything was blissful and most delightful; all curtains perfectly still and no sign of this eerie presence or its destructively dark drawing fear.

Having arrived here and thinking that I had maybe escaped and had found a peaceful abode, I was now unsure that this would be the case.

Most people kept themselves to themselves and there appeared to be some level of decency. Well, at some level anyway.

But then as the months passed by and the chinks of the true spirit of this place became all too apparent, this oh-so-perfect idyll was just a salacious bed of gossip, a place more Chinese than China with its tawdry whispers.

As I sat on that bench on the village green that day, I caught my first curious glimpse of one of the Curtain Twitchers in action. My eyes firmly fixed on this erratic curtain dance, each time revealing a little bit more of the identity of the Twitcher. Slowly turning around I then glimpsed two more Twitchers in action. It reminded me of some tribal ritual or a secret code being passed through the flapping and strange behaviour of the eccentricities of the human nature.

Oakley Place was a pleasant enough place but as you may expect there was quite an eclectic mix of individuals living here. It was a cross between those born and bred here and, as we were known, the interlopers. In certain places in the village I had sensed that there was a love-hate divide between the two categories of villagers. Generally, the main of the village folk were the salt of the earth and just as you would expect. However, as predictable as you may assume, you also had to contend with a minority of the high and mighty or the downright lost in the gene pool types.

I had decided to make a few enquiries into this strange phenomenon, and I had planned to meet old Major Buttertone-Smithe at the old village pub on Friday lunchtime which was apparently a good time and you were less likely to create any gossip. As the week raced ahead and Friday hastily approached, a whole array of momentous encounters ensued.

On Tuesday I had been stopped by Margaret Pemberton, the Parish Clerk, who had asked if everything was okay and had uttered, "Don't be drawn in by too much gossip, it's not as bleak here as you suspect."

At that point I stopped her and said, "What do you mean, Ms Pemberton?"

She plumped herself up and looked around her suspiciously. Suddenly I suspected that there might have been something more to her response. Ms Pemberton then reached fervently into her rather oversized bag and pushed a bunch of dried leaves with something attached to them into my hand forcefully.

She leaned towards me and whispered, "Put these in a safe place now. Do not look at what they reveal until you are safely behind closed doors."

I took a step back feeling slightly baffled and a little perplexed. I said, "Thank you, Ms Pemberton. It was lovely to see you today. I do hope we can chat again soon."

Across the road I had spotted not one but two curtains fluttering and then I had noticed Martin Fothergill, the gardener from Leverstone Manor, heading in my direction, or that quite possibly could have been in Ms Pemberton's direction. Ms Pemberton hurriedly picked up her bags and rushed off without pausing for thought and crashed headlong into Martin Fothergill, who was looking rather stern and had started raising his hands menacingly at Ms Pemberton. I then heard an incredibly loud explosion of sound which seemed to echo through the trees. At that point I was distracted and did not see the heated argument taking place between Mr Fothergill and Ms Pemberton on the High Street.

I had gone hurtling forward to try to see where this explosion of noise was coming from and as I ventured down the High Street and on to Pip Lane I looked back to check that Ms Pemberton was okay. I couldn't see her but strangely I saw Mr Fothergill heading back in the direction he had come from, carrying one of the bags that Ms Pemberton had been carrying. At the time I thought no more about it, as it was known that Martin Fothergill and Margaret Pemberton had been involved in a love triangle for a good while. It was also quite common practice for them to air their dirty linen in public for all to see.

Although feeling slightly perplexed I continued down Pip Lane, moving closer to the cacophony of sound. I had unexpectedly been joined by a group of boy scouts and their leader in charge, Harold Prestwick. Harold Prestwick, a pillar of society and an all-round good egg, had been trying to stem the noise of the over exuberant rabble he was trying to control. Harold had been involved with all the village groups at some point in his life. He was small and plump, well-kept and pleasant with a jovial demeanour. We all headed further down Pip Lane towards John Yarrow's farm, from where it seemed the noise was emanating.

Right before us, sprawled across the Yarrow's family farm, were camped a travelling circus and funfair. Harold and I went off to find John Yarrow, to ask him about this tomfoolery and what had possessed him to allow this bunch of strangers to pitch up in Oakley Place. As we looked for John Yarrow, we encountered the ringleader of this rabble, Frederick de Soames, who was busily bundling an oversized holdall into his Romany wagon. He was speaking in French to a rather petite and enchanting female who I believe he called Flora-Bella.

As we approached Frederick de Soames, he hurriedly turned tail and started heading in the opposite direction, rather like a startled hare that had been snared by a cunning hunter trapping its prey.

I shouted after him, "Have you seen John Yarrow?" but Harold Prestwick and I were met with a stony silence. Frederick de Soames was acting very oddly, and had now amassed an angry mob that was propelling itself in our direction.

Then very absurdly we noticed Penny Yarrow, John Yarrow's wife, and his daughter, Silvia, helping a large lady sporting a purple tutu into an elaborate headdress. I waved at Penny and Silvia to try to get their attention but they seemed to be caught up in something very odd.

Harold and I started making a hasty retreat towards John Yarrow's farmhouse, hoping to find John Yarrow. As we moved carefully towards the farmhouse door, we felt slightly alarmed — the door was wide open and the small stained-glass window in the top of the door had been smashed into razor-sharp shards, which had splintered and now glimmered on the ground beneath my feet. I suddenly heard a piercing scream and felt an icy chill move across me, causing a sickening sensation in my stomach.

I tried to turn to run. Harold had already bolted and was running away as fast as his legs would enable him, shouting that he was going back to call for the police. My feet were anchored firmly to the ground; I was trapped in the full clinch of terrifying fear. A rush of blood swirled around my body and my heart was beating like a million galloping horses racing towards the finish line. I reached behind me and grabbed a large walking stick that was leaning against the side of the door in an old antique umbrella stand. The walking stick was heavy and carried weight, which I thought might be useful in the event of coming face-to-face with the perpetrator of the terror beneath my feet. As I moved slowly towards the cellar door I could hear the heavy footsteps of someone pounding up the cellar flagstone steps. I quickly hid behind the old dresser, which I had helped John Yarrow move in front of the old inglenook fireplace last winter as the wind had been billowing down the chimney.

The cellar door creaked open, and a figure dressed in black lurched from the doorway. He turned and shouted down to the silence below. I heard a faint whimpering sound and then I heard the clatter of tin cans being knocked over. The figure dressed in black ran through the farmhouse door, not stopping to check what had caused the noise. I moved towards the cellar door cautiously, the feeling of fear was starting to engulf me again, and beads of sweat trickled down my face.

I called down into the depths of the cellar, "Who is there? Are you okay?" There was a muffled whimper in return. Flight and fear overwhelmed me. I ran down the flagstone steps carrying the walking stick like a tribal spear above my head. As I reached the bottom step, I could see a man gagged and bound to an old wooden milking stool. I could also see a small pool of blood trickling down from his wrist. I moved forward and bent down towards the figure tied to the stool. I was shocked but I assured the man that he was going to be fine. I removed the gag from his mouth and the blindfold that had been tied sickeningly tight to his frail skin, causing it to tear. I quickly tried to stem the blood trickling down from his wrist with an old lining cloth, which I had in my coat pocket. I wiped away the dirt, which had been ground into his face, and to my horror discovered that this frail man was John Yarrow.

He was fragile and looked as if he had not been fed a decent meal for more than a week. I found an old lantern and a box of matches, and quickly proceeded to light the lantern hoping to find an answer to my numerous questions and a way out of this fear-riddled place.

John Yarrow pointed to a pile of old newspapers that had been neatly stacked on a dusty pile of boxes near the foot of the steps. A mouse suddenly scuttled across the dusty pages throwing up a cloud of dust into the stifling air. The air was filled with a stench of blood, stale sweat and urine.

Poor John Yarrow gasped and grabbed hold of my arm as he begged me for water and something to eat. I scrabbled around and found a bottle of water. I removed the cap and handed the bottle carefully to John, who was gulping the water down like a desperate traveller thirsting from his wanderings in the desert.

I then heard the police sirens and suddenly at the top of the stairs I saw Police Officer Ben Greene shining his torch down the stairs. I called to him and asked him to call for an ambulance as well.

PC Greene said, "Who's down there?"

I shouted up to him, "It's me, Barney Lumsden. I've found John Yarrow. He is in a dreadful state and needs to get to the hospital as quickly as possible. He's lost quite a bit of blood and is extremely frail. Please hurry."

I heard PC Greene on his walkie-talkie calling for additional assistance; he had also asked for the police sniffer dogs to be brought over from across the Hertfordshire border. Another voice had now chorused down the stairs, but this time it was the recognisable tones of Harold Prestwick, who was talking to someone else upstairs and explaining how we had both arrived at John Yarrow's farmhouse that day.

Meanwhile PC Greene was hurriedly descending the flagstone cellar steps, while shining his torch around looking for clues as to why John Yarrow had been held in his own cellar. PC Ben Greene came towards us, and as he did he shone his torch around the dusty cellar. He stopped and placed his torch on the stacked boxes and took his black notebook from his uniform top pocket. He wrote down a description of the cellar, and noted all the points of interest like a cocked shotgun, which had been left pointing in the direction of John Yarrow. PC Greene also noted the blood and examined the gag and blindfold, placing them securely in plastic evidence bags. He then bent down on one knee and spoke to John Yarrow and questioned him on his capture. He also asked John Yarrow why the travellers were residing on his land. It appeared that everything that had been happening over the past few weeks was linked. And this also included the Curtain Twitchers, who were they and what was going on? It was all starting to look a little sinister and black.

I could hear Harold Prestwick upstairs talking to an unfamiliar voice and then we heard the rush of bodies as the paramedics came hurtling down the cellar steps with their equipment. I moved out of the way and PC Greene backed away and started to survey the cellar and look more in depth for clues. Two further police officers and a dog handler had also joined him with his sniffer dog. The paramedics were busy attending to John Yarrow, hooking him up to all manner of equipment. One of them called for further assistance while the other was calmly talking to John Yarrow.

I took this as my cue to vacate the cellar, and start a little bit of my own investigation work. I asked PC Greene if I could leave the scene but he seemed to be engrossed in the gun and a jagged blade that had been angled like a trap at John Yarrow's feet.

I ran hastily up the flagstone cellar steps and exited the cellar door, relieved to be away from the terror below.

Upstairs I was greeted by Harold Prestwick and Reginald Winterbottom, the farmhand who had been away on his holiday and had just pitched up to work back on the farm. I explained the chaos below and described how I had found John Yarrow. Harold looked horrified and then said that he had just passed Penny and Silvia Yarrow with Frederick de Soames. His face was white and he was trembling so I got him to sit down at the farmhouse kitchen table. Reginald filled the kettle to boil some water for a strong cup of tea. Reginald then joined us while he waited for the water to boil.

He said, "It's really odd; I went to check on the cows down at the top end field but they had been moved. I didn't think much of it though as I knew John Yarrow may have brought them in early for milking. But when I walked by the milking shed they were not there either. I did see a lot of blood splattered around and a few entrails, which I thought was a little odd as John would never have harmed any of the herd. After all, they are a prizewinning dairy herd, when all's said and done."

I paused momentarily and then asked, "Do you know anything about Frederick de Soames and the travellers pitched up with the circus and funfair overtaking the bottom fields leading into Oakley Place?" I asked Reginald if John Yarrow had mentioned anything at all about the strangers and why they were on the farm and now filtering into the local community.

Reginald said, "Well, yes, when I come to think about it, there was a day about three weeks ago. I had stayed over in the spare room as we had to make an early start for lambing. I heard Silvia having a heated argument with her dad about a group of people she had met down at the Jolly Hunter pub. Voices were raised and I did hear Silvia mention something about running off to join a circus and that her dad had better watch out, his time would come. Penny Yarrow, John's wife, had also joined in and seemed to have an axe to grind towards her husband that night too. Everything suddenly stopped and all I heard then were doors being banged closed. I went back to bed at that point, and thought no more about it. Do you think this had anything to do with why they're pitched up on the farm and why John Yarrow is down in the cellar?"

Just at that moment the shrill kettle whistle blew, shattering the silence in the kitchen. PC Greene and the other police officers came through the cellar door followed by the paramedics carrying a frail and incoherent John Yarrow on a stretcher towards a waiting ambulance that an attendant had flung open the doors to, as they hurriedly placed John Yarrow inside. We heard the paramedic in charge say that it was a life or death situation, and they had asked PC Greene to provide an escort off the farm and to join them on their journey to the local hospital. I stopped PC Greene to ask him some questions and to field some advice about the travellers.

PC Greene spoke briskly and said, "My prime concern at this present moment is to get John Yarrow safely to hospital."

The policeman gestured to the ambulance driver to get moving as he hurriedly got into his police car. PC Ben Greene wound down the window and leaning out asked, "I don't suppose you have seen anything odd happening around the village green lately?"

I was just about to start talking to him about the Curtain Twitchers, when he sped off in front of the ambulance, both hurtling forward at full speed, their sirens penetrating the silence of the countryside.

# Chapter Two

# The Madness

Barney turned back to Reginald and spoke to Harold who seemed to have perked up and was rummaging about in the biscuit barrel looking for a digestive or hob-nob to dunk in his tea.

Harold said, "Funny old day today, isn't it? Did you know that old Mrs Simpkins has not been seen in the post office for days? No one seems to have seen or heard anything from her. And Margaret Pemberton, the village clerk, has mysteriously vanished too."

I said, "Don't you think that's a bit odd, two people disappearing just like that?"

We looked at each other and then towards Reginald who was staring through the window, his gaze fixed on the circus and funfair. He was silent and seemed to be transfixed. Suddenly he spun around and beckoned me towards the window. He was panic-stricken and was starting to shake. He opened his mouth and spluttered that he had just seen Frederick de Soames and a few of the odd bunch of strangers bundling shrouded packages into his gypsy-style caravan.

He said, "Did you see that? Look! Look, there they are again. Oh no, what are they doing now?" He suddenly crouched down and grabbed hold of his stomach raising his hand to his mouth as if to stop himself being sick. "I cannot believe what I have just seen. We have to do something. Come on, we've got to get out of here before they get us too."

I said, "Reginald, slow down, what did you see? What's wrong with you? Slow down."

He grabbed his coat from the chair and picked up his bag shouting, "Quick, get out of here! We don't have time to hang about; we need to get back to the village as quick as we can!"

He started pointing towards the village and there were plumes of smoke billowing up. There was an acrid smell; a mixture of buildings and bodies, it was horrendous. Then we saw flames shooting up, filling the sky with blood-red light. Harold and I gathered our belongings, and raced towards the door; we then looked towards the funfair and circus tent and saw a large wooden figure blazing, as it stood high against the late afternoon sun. We glimpsed some strange depraved behaviour going on, some kind of bizarre ritual was occurring. There was a deafening chanting coming from the crowd, which was amassing around the burning figure, which rose from the lower end field.

Harold and I slammed the farmhouse door shut behind us and raced after Reginald who was trying to jump the fence.

We just about managed to catch up with him as I asked, "Reginald, what did you see? Please tell me, what exactly did you see?"

He stopped in his tracks and replied, "I think I know where Margaret Pemberton and Mrs Simpkin are. Don't you see? I cannot bear it anymore." He seemed to stumble again as if he was going to be sick. He stuttered, "They are, oh no, I can't say it, it's too sick for words. We have to get to the village and warn them. Please, can we go?" Harold had bent down and was scrabbling about in the dirt.

"What are you doing, Harold?"

"I saw something down there, moving in the bushes."

He pointed down towards the bushes that lined the perimeter edge of the field. We then heard a whispered voice coming from the direction of the bushes; there were then more than one muffled voice. Harold backed away slowly from the bushes; we then saw a bony hand reaching out through the base of the lower shrubbery. Reginald had stopped and was vomiting heavily. He then stopped and pointed towards the cowshed. There hanging like washing that had been pegged out to dry were two of John Yarrow's prizewinning cows, blood dripping from their lifeless carcasses.

We heard the muffled voices again and there slowly dragging through the bushes was a dishevelled and frail frame. The figure stumbled forward and stooped before us. It looked up at us and said, "Get out of here while you can, there is no time, no time, get out, get out!"

Harold and Reginald were scrambling over the fence, Harold shouted, "Barney mate, get out of there, get out! Quick, look over there, we've got to get out now!"

I turned around slowly to see an angry mob heading in our direction. They were not just angry, they seemed livacious and crazed.

Engorged with fear we cleared the fence and ran frantically towards the village green. Each step violently tracked by our pursuant, and each beat of our hearts pulled us further forward.

Harold suddenly stopped abruptly, his breathing erratic and stifled. As he gasped for air he muttered, "What do we do when we get to the village green? The police will be well out of sight by now."

I looked behind Harold at the mob edging closer at an incredible speed. I gestured to Harold and Reginald that we should hide behind the bales of hay as I did not think we could get to the village green now without being captured. If we hid behind the hay bales, the mob would hopefully not notice us as they passed us.

We dragged and stacked three hay bales to look as if they had been toppled, and crawled into the centre of them.

The sound of our pursuers grew louder, and we could feel their terror burying itself beneath our skin. Looking at each other in biting fear, with sweat streaming down our faces, we sat in silence not daring to breathe. We heard the thunderous footfall rushing by like a derailed train hurtling towards its doom. The terrifying chanting seemed to echo through the trees, growing deafeningly louder and hideously laden with the stench of death. The mob passed by and headed towards the village green. I could see smoke billowing up amongst the trees and the air was filled with an acrid smell.

Harold Prestwick and Reginald Winterbottom gathered our belongings together. We needed to find a way to get to the village green to see what the mob was up to.

Harold suggested, "We could find out if Jasper Swift is at home. I'm sure that he wouldn't mind if we hid in his attic. The attic window looks down onto the village green, and it would be the safest bet for us."

Reginald and I looked at each other nodding.

Reginald asked, "But how are we going to get to Jasper's without those monsters seeing us? I feel sick at the thought of any of us being captured by them." Reginald had turned ashen white and was shaking, sweat-filled fear rushing down his sodden face.

We all edged closer to the houses lining the perimeter of the village green, each step tentative and injected with a suffocating fear. When we heard frantic footsteps we dived for cover behind bushes and into ditches in desperation and sheer determination that we would not be caught by those perpetrators of terror. Slowly we seemed to gain momentum and were closing in on the front gate of

Jasper's house. I'm not sure how but we reached his front door and rasped the front door knocker.

After a few attempts and starting to feel that all hope was lost and with our anxieties rising fast we tried one last time; internally each of us was praying for some sweet divine intervention. Then the miracle of miracles occurred and Jasper flung wide his door and hurried us into his living room. Mrs Stanton was busy putting out food and brewing cups of tea in rapid succession as if it was going out of fashion. Jasper got us to sit down; he had drawn down the blinds and had closed all the shutters, so no one passing by could peer in or would know if Jasper was around. Jasper had bolted all the doors, and had propped his shotgun against the front door, as if to act as a deterrent against those parasitic avengers.

We could hear the hurried footsteps and the doors slamming shut along the lane and around the village green. Then all fell silent; an icy chill filled the air. We all looked at each other curious as to the stilted silence. Harold and Reginald ran upstairs panting and nervously peering between the slats of the blinds to observe the activity building silently below. Dark shadows were growing outside like a swarm of bees, dark and deadly, stalking their prey. We were the sitting ducks I feared and time was our master, shielding us from this pending terror.

Harold shouted down to us, "There's something a bit odd going on out there. I can't see clearly."

Then Reginald hurtled downstairs, dripping with sweat and panting madly. Once he had regained his breath he slowly said, "Is there anywhere we can hide?"

Jasper and Mrs Stanton shook their heads. Then in a flash of inspiration they pointed firstly to the boarded cellar door then up towards a metal door, which concealed an old attic room, which had been condemned as being a fire hazard, hence the metal door concealing its access. Jasper disappeared down the back passageway near the old utility room. We could hear him moving boxes frantically as he searched hurriedly for something to either prise the metal door away or break down the boarded cellar door. Reginald and I joined him and we were shortly joined by Harold. Mrs Stanton looked on petrified, her hands shaking as she hid between the lighted doors in the dark corridor.

It felt strange: here I was behaving like one of those deranged characters I had been watching for all those months and weeks. I was eager to see what was happening outside the security of our bolthole. As the blackness of the night enveloped the walls of the house, all was not as it should be below the window. I could see bright headlights, which blazed lighting the darkness of the night. The silence was shattered by the sound of an explosion; the glass in the window rattled and the house seemed to shudder.

I pressed my back against the bedroom wall, stealing glances through the slats to observe what was happening outside the window; I was eager to find out what had caused the explosion. The house across the way was blazing like a furnace, flames illuminating the blackness of the night. I could see hooded figures manhandling the occupants from their burning homes into a large covered wagon. There seemed to be people being bundled in like cattle, and then I spotted Frederick de Soames with his henchman cowering in the shadows. Then I saw them lurching in and out of the shadows, as they peppered the air with gunfire, startling the bats and waking the rooks from their parliaments.

There was then a loud pounding noise at the front door, and the house seemed to have been lit up like a Christmas tree. I ran downstairs. Harold, Reginald, Jasper and Mrs Stanton were quickly climbing through the hole they had made in the cellar door. I pelted forward and frantically squeezed myself through the gap. Once everyone was through we started to throw whatever we could find to conceal our whereabouts. One by one we stumbled down the cellar steps, trying to be as quiet as we could. There was a sudden explosion above us and we could hear heavy footsteps pounding the floors above our heads. The stench of death seemed to permeate the air and hang in the ether like a malevolent Spectre.

In hushed tones we tried to communicate with each other, feelings of fear and our pending doom all too clear. We could hear the heavy thuds of footsteps crashing above our heads, and we could smell the stale smell of death, which hung in the air like an ungrateful spirit. The sound of the pendulum in the old grandfather clock, which stood majestically in the hallway, clanked back and forth, its rhythmic pattern echoing through the silence.

With hearts racing we spoke in stilted whispers, fearful of the intruders above our heads. We froze and retreated deeper into the well of the cellar as we sensed movement on the other side of the hole. In silent plea-filled prayer, we asked for deliverance from our impending fate.

Just then we heard a loud commotion above followed by hurried footsteps rattling along the passageways. Then one by one each step fell silent, as if waiting, baiting our every turn. We waited and waited, in anticipation of what we suspected may happen next.

Time clicked by slowly.

Then, as the grains of sands rushing through the sands of time, the noise above dispersed and there was nothing but an eerie silence.

# Chapter Three
# A Broken Man

John Yarrow lay broken; his body was attached to bleeping machines, his fragile form a portion of his former self, motionless and etched with sadness. PC Greene looked on through the door of the intensive care unit, as nursing staff dutifully raced to save lives and bring reassurance to anxious families. The police were now scouring the surrounding villages for the offenders.

Back in Oakley Place, things had escalated: Frederick de Soames and his rabble were spreading out, staking their claim to new ground.

They had also set up camp near the village green, and were spreading like a veracious virus, blighting all in its wake.

'**Barney Lumsden**': the name was written in bold across the enquiry notes of PC Greene's notebook.

Deep in the cellar Mrs Stanton, Jasper, Reginald, Harold and I were tentatively moving things away from the hole that we had hastily made in our panic to hide from Frederick de Soames and his reprobates. Dust covered layers and clouds of thick smoke drifted through the clearing hole in the cellar wall. Feeling dazed and unstable we stumbled through the opening, uncertain what was waiting for us on the other side. Days had passed, each second a flicker of a dissipating flame. The air was heavy and hung like a soup of honey, which dripped and pulled air with each stilted breath.

Out in the lane and on the High Street all was silent; no bird song, no familiar sounds, even the clock had been silenced. Even the trees hung like lifeless forms devoid of life and meaning. Front doors of houses had been left wide open, windows smashed, fragments of glass glistened against the parched ground.

Jasper brushed the dust from his clothes and looked towards the others as they regained their composure.

"Barney, I'm staying put here with Mrs Stanton. I want you, Reginald and Harold to raise the alarm. The coast seems pretty clear at the moment, and if you go around to the old courtyard you'll find my old Morris Minor. The keys are hidden in-between the wheel arch and the back tyre. I'm going to barricade myself and Mrs Stanton in the house and hope they'll not be back. The three of you need to get to the town and alert the local police."

Barney, Reginald and Harold gazed at Jasper and Mrs Stanton, who looked weary and frail. The three of them were reluctant to venture any further, fear gripping their arms, and legs bound heavy and motionless to the ground.

Venturing forward, the three heard the heavy thud of Jasper's front door bang hard behind them; the clank of bolts being deadlocked, metal being thrown across steel locks. They fervently looked around them to survey their path to the old courtyard. Each sound was a reminder of the impending terror that might be encountered. What if they were spotted by Frederick de Soames or one of his entourage?

On reaching the courtyard they realised why Jasper had hidden his Morris Minor there: it was a perfect place, peaceful and forgotten. Ivy wound around the crumbling walls, which acted as a blanket shielding it from public view. The old Morris Minor stood hidden beneath rickety struts, remnants of an old stable. Barney located the keys, while Harold and Reginald cleared the foliage, which clung to the doors and windows of the Morris Minor. Jasper had quite clearly not used the vehicle recently, the smell of stale body odour imprinted on the worn cracked leather. Once Harold had cleared the fallen branches and densely covered path it was easy to move the car forward. The doors of the old Morris Minor creaked open noisily, rusted and crumbling metal held together by dirt and spider webs.

Driving slowly, we moved out of the old courtyard and observed the High Street to check if it would be a safe passage. The only other way out of the village was past John Yarrow's place, and that was a definite no-go area. We bundled ourselves into the car, crouching low in our seats, and drove steadily out of the courtyard, watchful in case we were noticed. Moving slowly down the High Street we passed Jasper's front door and glanced momentarily at the curtains around the green. There at the Buttertone-Smithe's the curtains twitched, and then I noticed others all seemingly springing to life; a dance of curtains, beating out a code across the green. We could not stay to find out more as we drove silently out of the village.

Turning to Harold and Reginald, I asked, "What do you think that's all in aid of, all those curtains flapping like that? A bit odd, don't you think?"

Harold and Reginald looked at each other knowingly as if they knew all about this strange behaviour. They were strangely silent.

Then Harold said, "You see, Barney mate, this is an old custom around here: when the place was rife with the plague that was the only way to get a message to each other."

Barney looked puzzled and couldn't help but ask a barrage of questions, each one firing from his lips like exploding bullets. "Okay, if that's the case why is it still happening? Can't people just text or call on their telephone or mobile?"

Harold and Reginald both laughed heartily. Barney felt a sudden belt of fear and gulped hard, not liking the sound of what was likely to come next.

Harold and Reginald both said in unison, "You see, the thing is, there's no need for all this new fangled gadgetry here. Not many folks here have mobile phones, computers or telephones. So that's why most village folk hate newcomers infiltrating our village. And when things start getting bad and the interlopers start trying to change village life, like putting in broadband and telephone boxes, well, that's when Frederick de Soames and the circus come to visit, isn't it? And usually after a few days of them being here everything tends to get back to normal."

Barney gripped the steering wheel, his hands warm and wet with fear slid around the leather steering wheel like water over ice. Barney spoke slowly to Harold and Reginald, "So you both know what's going on, don't you? Why have neither of you said what the big secret is? Why all the mystery?" Barney was on a roll; he asked question after question: "So you've both known about Frederick de Soames and the circus?"

Barney then stopped. He could see flashing police lights blazing ahead of him and was now eager more than ever to get to the safety of the police car. After all, the two people travelling with him were not who he thought they were. All this time he had been building an allegiance with Harold and Reginald and all along they had known about everything. Barney felt sickened and alarmed at this new discovery. What else had they been hiding from him? After all, they had not been at all honest and had been playing him for a fool all this time. But what should he do? Stay with Harold and Reginald or go it alone? His options were few and it was always better to keep your enemies close.

I stopped the car and pulled up behind the police car.

Harold and Reginald were in deep conversation and totally oblivious to the fact that the car had stopped. The police officer was on his walkie-talkie. I walked slowly towards the police car trying to catch the police officer's attention. I knocked on the window of the vehicle trying not to startle the driver.

The officer wound down the window and looked up, "Ah, it's you, Barney. It's good to see you, must have been reading my mind; we have been looking for you to ask you some questions, if we may."

The other police officer stepped out from the car and opened the rear passenger door, sternly instructing Barney to get in.

"I just wanted to know if there was any news on John Yarrow?"

Barney asked his question a second time looking worried as they bundled him into the police car.

"Well, Mr Lumsden, what can we say? It appears that ever since you arrived in Oakley Place there have been a large number of horrendous events occurring in these parts."

Barney felt sick as they reeled off the list of incidents.

"Well, what do you have to say about all that's been going on then?"

Barney was stunned and turned to look behind him out of the rear window of the police car. He could see Harold and Reginald; they were moving positions in the Morris Minor, and it looked like they were debating which one of them was going to drive. Frantically Barney tried to attract their attention as the other police officer had stepped from the police car and was approaching the Morris Minor.

Harold had planted himself in the driving seat, and Reginald sat next to him in the passenger seat. The police officer signalled to Harold to drive on. I looked on hoping that Harold would stop and ask what I was doing in the police car. Harold put his hand up and gave a signal, and the next second he drove off leaving me behind in the police car.

# Chapter Four
# Close Kept Secret

The officer got back into the police car while the other officer leaned across and put a cloth, which had been heavily coated in some kind of tranquiliser, over my mouth.

I felt strange and my limbs felt heavy, I tried desperately to stay awake. I felt a sudden sensation of speed and then the feeling of being dragged across a cold floor. The faint smell of ammonia hit my nostrils and gave a jolt to my senses. As they continued to drag me across the floor I pretended to be out cold. The dragging stopped and my body was lifted on to a wooden bench, sharp splinters of broken wood dug into my back. I wanted to scream, but refrained from blowing my state. I waited until I heard the heavy thud of the door slamming closed.

I carefully opened my eyes and peered around the room. The smell was pungent, decaying clothes piled untidily in a damp corner of this pokey room. The windowpane was cracked and heavy with dirt, locked tightly. The air was stifling and as I gasped for air, I knew I had to find a way of getting out of this place. I stumbled to my feet, looking around the room for an escape route. The door was heavy and barred with metal poles. I heard the sound of heavy footsteps on the other side of the door, and shouts, which echoed around this miserable place. The footsteps had abruptly stopped on the other side of the door. I bolted and lay back on the wooden bench as if out cold, not daring to move, trapped in frozen fear. The metal pole banged and clattered to the floor as the door sprang open.

A figure dressed in a white coat came in. I peeked momentarily but I could not tell if it was a man or a woman. This being had been followed in by two others, who I could not see clearly. One of them placed a bag over my head while the other tied up my hands and feet. I felt them lift me and carry me down a draughty corridor. There were screams echoing all around me and I could feel myself falling unconscious again. The smell was repulsive, and I felt glad for the bag over my head protecting me from the full intensity of this odour.

I felt them push me upright onto a metal chair, the icy chill of the cold metal hard on the small of my back. A sharp stab in my left arm, and my head hit the desk that I had been wedged in front of. The thud of my head hitting the metal desk brought me to my senses. I must have yelped as the bag was pulled off my head and a bright light was flashed into my eyes, its heat and intensity unbearable.

A voice boomed out through a speaker on the wall, while something lurked behind me shrouded in black, its breath pungent and unpleasant, rasping as it moved erratically behind me. My arms and feet were still tied, but at least I could breathe now without the bag over my head.

The voice crackled through the broken speaker, which hung free from the wall, "Mr Lumsden, thank you for finally cooperating with us. We have been waiting for you to come to your senses."

Barney paused and gulped. He was not sure how to respond. The voice was not clear, yet so familiar.

"Who are you? What do you need from me? What are you going to do with me?"

Barney stopped.

Silence engulfed the room.

The voice repeated the questions and demanded Barney's response. "We have brought you here for your own safety. We apologise for our approach. Do you know who we are now and why you're here, Barney?"

I tried to speak, the words trapped in the back of my throat, "What do you want from me? How do you know me? Please tell me who you are and why I'm here. If you're friends, please let me go, I need to help the others. Time's running out for us all. I'm not sure why I'm saying this to a glass wall, especially when I do not know who you are. So, tell me who are you are, please, I beg you."

There was a flurry of activity. I had not realised that there had been a second person in the room, who had been sat in the darkness, obscured by a heavy screen, which had been drawn across a corner of the room. A piercing screech echoed around the room as the screen was pulled across the floor, etching heavy grooves into the wooden floor. The voice boomed through the speaker again, this time crystal clear and quite clearly the voice of Major Buttertone-Smithe.

Then from the darkened corner stepped a feminine form. "Do you know who I am, Barney? Is it all starting to become a little clearer?" spoke the voice out of the darkness.

"No. Please tell me who you are. I need to know or should I say we need to get going and get back to the village to help people like Jasper and Mrs Stanton, don't we?"

The female had stepped a little further into the room, the bright light casting a glowing halo around the her form, and with that came enlightenment as to who this stranger was. Stepping even closer it became clear that this was Ms Pemberton. But what was happening and why had they brought him here? Where was he and what was going on? These questions circled his mind like hungry vultures pecking his subconscious, each time chipping away fragments and creating ocean upon ocean of ever-expanding questions. Barney sat in stunned silence looking into the dark spaces, which pocketed the corners of the room, wondering if anyone else would be stepping from the shadowy dark recesses of the room.

The doorway was suddenly lit and a stout form stood blocking the light, fragments of the tweed-suited Major framed like a silhouette, masking his face as he leaned into the room. Ms Pemberton was now moving towards him, each step precise and ordered, purposeful and filled with conviction. Major Buttertone-Smithe entered the room drawing closer to Ms Pemberton. As the light hit them both, I noticed a talisman hanging around Ms Pemberton's neck and another dangling from the Major's jacket pocket. I suddenly remembered that day on the High Street when Margaret Pemberton had forced the leaves and something strange into my hand and told me not to look until I was safely behind closed doors. What with all of the cacophony of sound, the argument and everything else, I had quite clearly forgotten about it. I remembered diving through my front door and dropping these items into my partly opened drawer in the hallway dresser. I then left quickly and proceeded downstairs to find out where the noise was coming from. The rest was history, or was it?

"Barney, did you read my note and take the talisman, I gave you?" asked Margaret Pemberton.

Barney looked blank not knowing what to say for the best. He admitted, "No, I left it and don't know what you're talking about. What note and talisman?"

Margaret Pemberton clarified what Barney had secretly suspected.

She started to explain, "Do you remember that day on the High Street, the day I had that massive argument with Martin Fothergill, when I gave you the note and pressed the talisman into your hand? I had hoped that you would have read the note; I tried to warn you to get out while you could before they started their rampage through our village once again. Why did you not read it, Barney, why?" Her tone was agitated and angry, and she did not want to stop her questioning there.

Major Buttertone-Smithe had now pulled the facing chair from the desk and drew himself upright to plant himself down onto the chair. He leaned forward and his eyes scanned me, questioning everything. Ms Pemberton had silently stepped back into the shadows. The Major pulled a notebook from his pocket, and started making notes but every word was written in some bizarre code.

He then stopped and looking into my eyes said, "Barney, I bet you're wondering what all this madness is about, aren't you? Well, there are many things we need to make you aware of and explain. So, I'll begin at the beginning, shall I? Barney, Ms Pemberton and I are Government agents, who have been asked to investigate the strange disappearances of new residents of Oakley Place. People have been disappearing for centuries, but it seems to happen every time Frederick de Soames, the circus and his clan arrive in Oakley Place. After a short while we discover that nearly all of the interlopers have mysteriously vanished with no trace whatsoever. Then after a few days Frederick de Soames and his entourage pack up and just disappear, and everything resumes as normal, as if nothing has happened. The only people left, however, are the folks that have been born and bred there, no newbies or interlopers to be found anywhere."

Barney sat, his mouth gaping wide and motionless, his eyes searching in the curtained light for answers.

"So, you're telling me this is some kind of age-old occurrence that my arrival has triggered, are you? You must think I am bonkers, you really must. I am most definitely not though. Now tell me the real truth, and cut the crap. Tell me honestly why you've brought me here and what is really going on."

The Major turned to Ms Pemberton, "I just knew it. I said he'd be a hard nut to crack, didn't I, Ms Pemberton? Damn fool won't believe us will he until we give him hard proof." The Major paused then hesitantly beckoned the being that had been pacing behind me.

Margaret Pemberton and Major Buttertone-Smithe spoke in unison, "Well, we really did not want to show you this person, but we're afraid to say you've left us with little choice, Barney."

They beckoned the being again. This time there was some slow movement behind me and then I felt the rasping breath restless next to my right side. It moved into the light revealing its identity. Light now filtered through the dark shadows in every corner of the room.

As the being came into the light I noticed that it was in fact someone similar in stature to Martin Fothergill. I looked closer. The person seemed to shuffle and was covered from their head, and indeed the whole of their body, in pus-like sores. The smell was vile, and made me gag.

"This poor unfortunate is Martin Fothergill from Leverstone Manor. It appears that he was not born and bred in Oakley Place as everyone had presumed. Ms Pemberton had been trying to get him to leave. The day that she saw you on the High Street and you witnessed that argument was her telling him to leave. Well, he did not listen and he stayed. He even went to join in Frederick de Soames' strange rituals not realising that only those born and bred in Oakley Place were protected from the curse he brought each time. You see, Frederick de Soames had been a key figure in the great plague, since around about sometime in the 1340s. It appears that he had been infected with the plague, and that all of his family and most of this village had been decimated by death. At that time there had been an elderly couple that lived near the village green. They were known as wise folk and had laid a curse on Frederick de Soames and the whole village. The curse they placed was that whosoever came into contact with Frederick de Soames would surely perish if they were not protected by the talisman. Those persons not born and bred in Oakley Place were not protected as they did not possess the talisman that was given to each child born within the village on their day of birth. Messages had been passed throughout the village through the twittering and flittering curtains, and each time those protected by the talisman would be helped to warn the interlopers and newbies to get out quick. Sadly, most new folk never really understood what it was all about. That is, Barney, until you arrived. You see, because you had the talisman, you were automatically under its protection and not at risk. That's why you have not fallen sick so far, Barney. We have also injected you with a mix of antiviral herbs, which will protect you."

Martin Fothergill had shuffled back into the shadows, and the air was filled with mournful moans, which echoed around the corridors outside.

Margaret Pemberton moved forward and stood next to the Major, "I think the others are getting restless and it's a full moon tonight. We need to make sure they're all back in their rooms before midnight. It also means that we have to get back to the village and get any newbies out to safety, as Frederick de Soames and his clan will be back in the village to make their final cull."

I was desperate by now to leave. Through flickering shadows and strands of light I had just caught sight of the clock on the wall; its hands moving slowly towards 9:30 p.m. Margaret Pemberton had just said that it was Thursday. Had I been there for almost a week? I thought I'd only been there for a few days. What had they given me to knock me out for so long and why had I been left in that dreadful room? I also wondered if Harold and Reginald had got back to the village and what they were up to. Well, it appears my questions, or at least some of them, were about to be answered.

The Major and Ms Pemberton quickly left the room, and a man in a white coat entered the room, followed by two other men who had jointly moved towards Martin Fothergill hidden in the shadows. They placed manacles on his hands and feet, which must have caused him great pain as he let out a piercing scream. The man in the white coat appeared to insert a large hypodermic needle into Martin Fothergill's leg. Martin seemed to lurch forward and subsequently crumpled like a deck of cards before they lifted him and carried him out of the room.

As the man in the white coat exited the room, I asked, "Do you know where the Major and Ms Pemberton have gone?"

He retorted, "They're packing some equipment before they return to the village and I believe they're taking you with them. I can't stand here talking anymore; the inmates are growing restless." He seemed quite agitated and aggressive in his tone.

I was eager and hoping to ask more questions but he left at speed. The door of the room swung hard on its hinges. There was a faint smell of vomit wafting through the door, followed by a strong chlorine chemical type smell. I attempted to get up from my chair, but had forgotten that I was manacled to the desk.

Ms Pemberton then rushed through the door carrying an oversized bag. She called out to a guard in the corridor for assistance.

"Barney, I've just called the guard to get the keys, we need to get moving as soon as possible. Time's running out and the Major and I need to get you back to the village. There's no time to lose at all; time is of the essence. As soon as the Major arrives we'll be leaving. Once we have removed the manacles we need you to gather whatever you have before we leave."

The guard, balancing on one knee, unlocked the manacles. I moved my arms and legs trying to get my circulation flowing again. Metal indents left etched in my skin where the manacles had been, my skin was raised red and sore, rubbed to the point of bleeding. My eyes stung from a sudden blaze of light, as the lights glared from every corner of the room. My body ached and I suddenly felt the full pelt of hunger rip through my body making me feel faint and unable to move.

A second guard appeared with a plate of bread, cheese and a jug of water, slamming them down against the metal of the desk. My hands were shaking as I forced the bread and cheese into my dry mouth as fast as possible. I gulped down the water as if I'd been in a dusty desert for days.

The Major entered the room with great authority. He gestured towards Ms Pemberton, who rushed to his side, and spoke to her in quiet tones. I looked on, wondering what was about to occur. I felt uncomfortable and anxious as I sensed great peril.

"Major Buttertone-Smithe, can you tell me why you need me to go back with you, please?"

The Major spun around to face me. He looked angry, "How dare you ask me such a nonsensical question like that, Barney lad? Do you not know that it's down to your arrival in Oakley Place that set this process in motion yet again? We had just recovered from a visit from Frederick de Soames some three weeks ago. Last time it was a young

French female called Flora-Bella. Frederick de Soames arrived rapidly that time; a majority of people were left well alone. She vanished, however, as quickly as the dense fog he brought that night. No one ever saw or heard of her again. Her family made enquiries to the Government and a few other agents were sent in to investigate. But alas nothing was found; no trace of her whatsoever. You, however, Barney, you are a different matter altogether. You hold a secret that I'm not sure even you are aware of. We've been watching you and monitoring your movements for the last ten years."

Barney sat stunned at this news; he had often sensed that he was being watched.

The Major stood up abruptly and said, "Well, we can't sit here chit-chatting all day and night; we have work to do and do it we will, with your help though, Barney. It's all down fairly and squarely to you; you're the only one here that holds the key and that's why we sought to bring you here to Banthom's Biological Laboratory. We have been testing some of the inmates to see if we can fathom a formula to manufacture an antidote. So far we've been, well, woefully unsuccessful, but we did take a strand of your DNA and we think we may have struck gold at long last."

All three were now getting ready to leave the Biological Laboratory. They were heavily loaded with all manner of gadgetry to plot and protect them. Anyone would have thought they were going into a war zone.

# Chapter Five

# The Darkness

A large armoured Jeep stopped at the entrance of Banthom's Biological Laboratory and a guard appeared wearing a biological warfare suit.

The Major handed me an overall and a mask, "Barney, we all need to put these on before we get back to the village; we think things have escalated rapidly while you have been away."

Barney stared at the Major and Ms Pemberton.

"What do you mean? What's happened? It was peaceful when I left with Harold and Reginald. We had set off for the local police station to report what was happening. However, well before we had a chance to do so we were flagged down by a police car. Harold and Reginald made their escape and I thought that maybe they had been heading back to the village as I had discovered that they knew about everything that had been happening."

The Major and Ms Pemberton were busily putting on their biological warfare suits so I took this as my cue to stop talking and put the overall on quickly.

The windows were blackened and tightly closed and the Jeep smelt of stale body odour and chemicals. There appeared to be a hive of activity in the vehicle, with computers buzzing and a soldier positioned at the back and front of the Jeep armed with guns. One was monitoring something on a screen; every time I tried to look I was pushed back into my seat. Ms Pemberton was on the phone, while writing down some kind of information. The Major was shouting orders at the driver and I sat in my seat nervously. They had not explained anything and I felt totally unprepared for whatever was going to happen.

The Jeep was travelling at speed now, and as we travelled I was determined to bombard them with questions.

"So Major Buttertone-Smithe and Ms Pemberton, what should I expect when we get back to the village? You have not told me anything all, and why is it so imperative that I return with you? Just exactly what is going on? I have to say I'm not looking forward to this one bit. Tell me what's going to happen and why, oh why, do you need me of all people? I really am no one that special, am I, seriously?"

Branches were hitting against the side of the Jeep at speed, rattling like ghostly chains. Was this just merely a precursor of what was to come, or was my fragile mind working overtime now?

The Major and Ms Pemberton scrabbled around in their files, and then threw one of the files across the Jeep to me. They said, "This should explain everything in a bit of detail, read it as quickly as you can and make sure you sign the last page as this is highly classified information. When you've finished, place it in this envelope and hand it to the soldier at the rear of the Jeep as you exit when we get to the village."

Ms Pemberton spoke briskly and said, "I have to warn you, Barney, that you may be shocked; some of what the file contains is not pleasant. You do not have very long, as we should be back in the village within the next hour so read as much as you can, do not take photos of anything and be sure not to reveal its contents to anyone."

The file read *'Confidential File of Barney Lumsden'*.

Written below this were a series of numbers and then a code of some kind. I opened the file tentatively, a little nervous as to what I may be about to discover. On the first page was information about my vital statistics, you know what I mean, hair colour, shoe size, all that useful sort of information you dread that anyone may find out about you, really personal stuff. The second page was quite detailed, listing information about all my family. I started to feel slightly invaded, and wondered if everyone had a file of this nature held by the Government in the UK. I continued leafing through each page, scanning every word, as if my life depended on every letter that had been written.

The driver shouted, "Heads down, everyone! Something's heading in our direction. I'm just going to pull into this lay-by ahead until it passes. They should not even see us as it's pitch black here"

"Okay, do what you have to, but don't take all day about it. Remember, we've got little time before ..." He looked at me and stopped.

Barney, continued thumbing through each page within the file, trying to find an answer. Looking up from the file, I said, "Major, what do you mean? Before what?"

The Major did not answer; he looked uncomfortable as he moved in his leather seat.

The Jeep then suddenly veered off towards the dense foliage of the bushes, cloaked in darkness at the road edge. We stopped in the bushes and as the vehicle ahead passed us by, the driver shouted out the number plate to the soldier positioned at the back of the Jeep. The soldier wrote it down and then seemed to process the information through his computer. He put up his hand as if to signal something, but said nothing and then carried on doing what he had been doing prior to the abrupt stop.

The whole Jeep seemed to fall under a spell of silence; there was a low hum of harmonics as the vehicle passed by. I tried to look through the clearing of the windscreen but my view was distorted. The soldier sitting in the front seat next to the driver had crouched down low, as had the driver. A second vehicle was in convoy with the first passing vehicle; it looked like a Romany wagon a little similar to that of Frederick de Soames.

As the wagon passed the Jeep, I saw grey shrouded figures lurching in the back. Then in one terrifying moment both vehicles stopped. I glimpsed an arm dangling out of the open door of the wagon. Lights started flashing around and it seemed as if one by one, the occupants of the vehicles were swarming like killer bees in our direction. We all hit the deck and lay in pitch-blackness; the windows of the Jeep were blackened out so anyone looking in would see nothing. As we lay absorbing the fear and the darkness both inside and out, the Jeep started to move in a rocking motion; it seemed as if they were trying to prise open the Jeep like a tin of cold meat.

The driver in his panic sat bolt upright and screamed, "Hold on everyone! It's going to be a bumpy ride!"

As he pelted forward at speed, we felt the thud of bodies smash against the chassis.

"It was either them or us, and I'm sure as hell not prepared to wait it out," spat the driver.

One by one we grappled to the safety of our seats, bashed, battered and bruised but relieved to have escaped, this time at least. The contents of the file were scattered and torn, jettisoned to every corner of the vehicle. Slowly picking up the pieces, I noticed two weird symbols on one of the torn pages. Moving back again to my seat after collecting the remnants of the file, I sat and studied these symbols. I'm not sure what they meant and Ms Pemberton had spotted me examining the symbols.

"Barney, it would be wise not to question the Major about those. All I can say is that is why you need to come back to Oakley Place with us."

I looked at her, wondering what she was talking about this time; nothing was making sense, least of all this. They were taking me back to Oakley Place to do something of great importance, as I held a mysterious secret. I was tired and losing patience; my head was thumping trying to piece all of this together. I had started to think that maybe I should have stayed back in the chaos of the Big Smoke. Although that journey had not been a bowl of cherries either, I'll try and fill you in on that at some point.

The road was heavily pitted and uneven as we were bashed along in the Jeep.

"It looks like all is quiet ahead, which is strange. I wonder where the guards are, Major," spoke an anxious sounding Ms Pemberton.

Then the Jeep started to lose speed, as it slowly drove towards a concealed roadblock ahead. Something flitted in the darkness, the trees swayed and there seemed to be one or two figures slowly moving between the densely wooded areas to one side of the roadblock. As we moved slowly, now almost slower than a speeding snail, the soldier at the rear of the Jeep was frantically trying to communicate with the guard supposedly guarding the checkpoint. He persistently attempted to make contact with the guard at the checkpoint, but was met with a chilling silence. He tried again and again but there was no response. Private Peterson tried one last time, determined as always to fulfil his task. At his final attempt we overheard faint screams of more than one person. There was a distinctive click and then a profound silence fuzzed through the airways.

We moved cautiously through the checkpoint, the soldiers flashing lights at either side of the road just in case we were being set up for a swift ambush. Then one of the figures we had spotted lurking in the darkness hit the bonnet of the Jeep.

I heard the impact, the Jeep jolted to one side and rocked as it tried to regain its balance and momentum. As the Jeep stopped, this figure that had perilously collided with the Jeep miraculously stood back stunned as if it had been tranquillised by a hunter. I looked through the window and noticed the clothes, which hung loosely on the plump figure, and at that point I realised that this was Harold Prestwick. He was dripping in a mixture of blood and sweat, his hands raised as if pleading to be rescued and beckoning wildly to another figure emerging at speed through the densely wooded area. The look of terror etched into their eyes, as they frantically banged their hands on the doors trying to get in. As I looked towards the densely wooded area, I noticed figures carrying flaming torches blazing through the blackness of the night.

I sat with my back pressed hard against the seat. Harold and Reginald were pleading and hammering hard against the Jeep. There was a sudden silence, followed by deathly screams of anguish.

I could not stand it any longer; I begged the Major and Ms Pemberton to let them in. But my words were unfounded; they looked past what was right in front of their line of vision.

"You've got to let them in, they're my friends. I know what they did was wrong but without them you would never have found me."

I noticed the torches moving closer, Harold and Reginald pressing harder against the glass. Their eyes filled with terror, perspiration dripping down their worn faces. As they held out their hands pleading for their lives, I could see the frailty of their skin hanging loose on broken bones. I could stand it no longer, and barged past Private Peterson, the soldier at the rear of the Jeep. He moved quickly to block my way, obviously aware that I was trying to get the back door of the vehicle open to let in Harold and Reginald.

Ms Pemberton surged forward from her seat and screamed, "No, Barney, no!" She lunged forward, grabbing wildly at my arms.

The soldier covering the back door of the Jeep pushed me back sharply, causing me to topple back like a weeble-wobble but instead of righting myself, I fell backwards, falling fast and hard, before landing sharp against the point of a hypodermic needle held out by Ms Pemberton. My body started to feel heavy and then, falling like a stone, I hit the deck, colliding rapidly with the metal of the floor. Voices echoed around me. I thought I heard the creak of metal like a car door opening. Each second the sound grew denser, the air around me heavier, my chest felt pinned as if a weight rested hard against me. A deadening silence, ebbed and flowed with each breathe in, air aching to escape my fractured body.

Barney was out cold barely breathing and fragmented holding on to strands of existence like a butterfly caught in a spinning wheel, fracturing with each cruel turn.

The back door of the Jeep opened, bloodied and wide.

Major Buttertone-Smithe sat bound and gagged, Ms Pemberton stood aggressively outside the door of the Jeep. Private Peterson lay face down, motionless, his clothing ragged and torn as if he had been attacked by bears, large tearing marks etched across his back. Both the driver and Sergeant Anderson, who had been seated in the front of the Jeep, were now following the demands and orders of Ms Pemberton.

The air outside of the Jeep was thick with smoke as flames shot through the air transcending the darkness. I was coming round gradually, my eyes opening slowly, fleetingly glimpsing a changing scene. The back of my clothes were damp and clinging to me like liquid tarpaulins, dragging me back heavily towards the ground as I tried to wrench myself from the ice-cold chill of the Jeep's metal carcass.

What was happening?

Fear gripped me and propelled me forward towards the door of the Jeep; I could hear muffled whimpers and the dulcet tones of Ms Pemberton. However, it was quite clear that there had been a bizarre sea change in my temporary absence. Blood splattered and speckled the white paintwork of the exterior of the Jeep, which was pitted with dents and the remnants of damaged bodies.

I moved steadily, trying to hide in the shadows, which rose and swirled around the atmosphere. I'm not one to panic but something was wrong, in stupendously epic proportions of monumental horror, which now spread out like a sea before me. There ahead of me, like towers of rising death, bodies piled one on one, the smell of decaying flesh, sickly sweet, fragranced by sadness. Ms Pemberton waded in through the bodies, as if sifting through the post left scattered on the steely floor tiles, oblivious to the fractured bodies underneath her concrete heels, which pounded against a black history. It was now starting to become clear that things were truly not how I had believed them to be. The perfect reasoning inside my brain, left shredded and scattered in my tired head. Turning quickly I noticed a crouching body hunched over as if protecting another.

Dodging the light given out by the torch of Ms Pemberton and the soldiers as they searched through the bodies, I'm not sure who or what they were erratically searching for in the sea of terror.

I was now crawling through the dirt, trying to stay low towards the ground. As I drew nearer to this crouching form, I noticed the clothes, which were tattered and heavy with blood. Cradled in the figure's arms lay another, someone familiar but not yet clear. I was now as close as I truly wanted or needed to be, our breath mingled together.

The person cradling the figure spoke and said, "Don't you remember me? You are Barney Lumsden, aren't you? I really hope that it's you. Please tell me that's you there, Barney."

Barney lost his balance momentarily, as he recoiled. "Who are you? I need to know and I cannot see you clearly."

The voice said, "It's Jasper and Mrs Stanton. They came back after you left. They bashed the door down; we panicked and ran back down to the cellar. They were like bloodhounds hunting us down like we were vermin they were trying to get rid of. That Frederick de Soames dragged us out full force and all, he's completely wicked, that one."

There was a chilled silence. I sat trying to understand. "Jasper, are you okay? What can I do to help? Is Mrs Stanton okay?" In the stillness my thoughts pounded in my head, like a derailed train flying erratically down a one-way track of impending doom. "Jasper, how did you both get here? We must be at least 15 miles away from the village."

Looking up at Barney, Jasper said, "Is that what you think? No, lad, we're much closer than that."

Barney looked around feeling slightly dazed by the whole experience. "What do you mean, Jasper? Where are we then?"

Trying to move Mrs Stanton to a comfortable position Jasper slowly shuffled, raising himself to his feet. He stood up and immediately embraced Barney as if he were a long-lost child. They both stood and scanned the scene around them; it was difficult to see amidst the piles of bodies, which were stacked high around them, like towers of solitude and despair. The mist and smoke wafted, and through intermittent clearings we caught glimpses of the true horror of what we would next discover. Through silent swirls of clouds, we glimpsed the High Street. Jasper had slumped back to his stopper and cradled Mrs Stanton in his frail arms.

I stared into the dusty air, hoping that what my eyes, which were heavy with tears skewing my clear sight, were now looking at what was just a mere illusion. My feet rooted to the spot, and my body anchored to this nightmare, I felt bizarrely complicit to everything that surrounded me. But this was absurd, as I had not been a willing participant, but a hijacked prisoner. A piece of a dark puzzle, lost in this half-life state.

This hellish nightmare was unfolding like a dogwart flower. Gripped in fear's fatal grasp, my body feeling slammed by the madness all around me. I had thought I had left these scenes behind me in my past.

This was like a killing field; my eyes were stinging with tears, my heart fragmenting with the vista before me.

# Chapter Six

# Fragmented Reality

In the distance, the High Street of Oakley Place was strangely picturesque, perfectly reminiscent of those picture postcards. The doors of each house wide open and welcoming, fragments of glass glistened in the dirt and scratched the earth below. The curtains flapped erratically just as they had done on that day on the village green. That day seemed so far away now, and yet it was all but a few days ago. Then like a bolt of fiery lightning I was hit and my body thudded and crashed to the ground.

As I tried to look up I felt a dark looming figure above me, blackness shriven in every pore, the stench of death hung upon his frame like a pungent fragrance. His eyes like blackened coals, features of his face looking as a ravaged hag in those old 'Hammer House' movies of yesteryear.

I could see the blackness in his soul, and the overwhelming pain of the night engulfing him like a shroud of vile terror. For above me this stark figure was no less than that of Frederick de Soames.

He leaned over me and swooped down, whispering and chanting. His breath stank of rotten bodies and stale air. Each time he opened his mouth I felt sick, the bile building in my throat before slinking back in fear.

Like an avenging angel we were joined by Ms Pemberton and two of the soldiers, their feet guarding my body, their guns pointing at Frederick de Soames as he rose to the fullness of his character. Then as if in some crazy dream, Frederick de Soames vanished, his presence no longer like a heavy ball and chain. Ms Pemberton leaned down and helped me to my feet. In her hand she held the talisman, as did the two soldiers. She threw down a talisman, which bounced off my chest as I grappled to my feet.

"Barney, what do you think you are doing?"

I gazed at her in disbelief, "What do you mean, Ms Pemberton? Can you not see the hell in this place? What does it all mean? What is really going on?"

There was a chilled silence; she turned away and stared around her, tears welling up in her eyes, the frustration and the madness of it all etched heavy on her brow.

"Barney, I just wish there was a way to stop this madness, we have been in this place so many times now. We come in and pick up the pieces. Each time the scale of the terror escalates and this time there are no words to describe our despair. I am weary and cannot fathom how we can bring this nightmare to its end. I had hoped you, Barney, were the key, the missing piece, the resolution to this nightmare, our knight in shining armour, here to rescue us all."

She gazed full of hope into Barney's eyes, her hands clasped on his hopeful and optimistic anticipation. She leaned into Barney and rested her head on his shoulder. Barney felt Ms Pemberton's breath on his cheek, and her head resting into his shoulder as though he were shielding her from this despair.

The two soldiers from the Jeep, were now joined by other soldiers who were diligently searching each and every corner of Oakley Place.

"What are they looking for, Ms Pemberton, and why are they going into each house? What are they looking for exactly?"

Ms Pemberton slowly moved and faced me full on, the tips of her shoes locking with mine. She placed her hands on my shoulders and said, "There are many, many things, Barney, that you need to know and understand about Oakley Place and your life. You are not here by some strange coincidence, all this is how it has been written and you are the key, as were your ancestors before you. I too am part of that key and that is why now we must work together to put this madness to death once and for all."

I stepped back, shards of glass cracking under my feet.

"Ms Pemberton, as I hold this talisman, it's all starting to strangely make sense, though I'm not really sure what it's all about. What do you mean, my ancestors? How were they involved in this? How are you part of this too? There are too many questions and not enough answers. I need to know everything right from the beginning of this madness, and what do you mean that it's written? Where is this written evidence?"

Barney stared questioningly; he wanted answers and these answers hung like heavy dew in the air around them. But time was eroding what fleeting remnants of hope they had left. Daylight was slipping away along with the answers, night would soon be upon them once again and time was evaporating any hope of a solution to this bad dream.

The soldiers were pounding in and out of each house, as if a tornado were ripping through the landscape of this peaceful idyll. They were throwing anything of interest into large piles in the centre of the village green, the pile of debris rising like a bonfire of pain.

Night was drawing in, wave on wave of bleakness, rolling in and out like tides of solitude and washing away with each ebb and flow the tranquillity and beauty of this beautiful village's heart. Ms Pemberton and myself teetering on the edge of impending doom, and yet we hoped that somehow we would surmount this insurmountable prison of hell. The colours of the day bleeding and running through the streets of Oakley Place, silently racked in a sea of anguish and left replete of joy. The question burning heavily on my lips was, who were the Curtain Twitchers, and what was indeed their message?

Barney and Ms Pemberton sat quietly watching every movement around them, noting each discovery made by the soldiers. As the night chill enveloped them where they sat, the icy cold pierced their bones, sending splinters of pain through their very beings.

Barney spoke softly to Ms Pemberton, who leaned once more into him, warming from his body heat like a loving protector. Slowly they rose as one to their feet, and moved off to the welcoming light of Jasper and Mrs Stanton's doorway that was open wide. As they approached the front door they looked at each other and both said, "I think tonight may be a long night, there is much to do, but first we must—"

They both stopped abruptly. For there before them lay bodies; they were not dead, though in mournful pain and stifled in deep sorrow. We kneeled down amongst them trying to find out who they were and why they were here of all places.

A child suddenly sat bolt upright and spoke. "Lady, lady, why are we here?" She pointed at Ms Pemberton and reached out towards the talisman hanging around Ms Pemberton's neck.

It was not until this point that I had clearly seen the talisman. In my curiosity I reached into my pocket and retrieved the talisman Ms Pemberton had given me earlier.

It rested in the palm of my hand, shiny and cold, a bold symbol on one side and on the reverse a message written in some strange language, none that I had seen before though it seemed to look like Latin.

The words etched on the talisman read as follows:

' *Umbrae protegat, quos hide, ex lumine sanctity affert, et lux a tenebris. Ipsae cadent, omnes qui, sub tutela, salvus erit.*' *(Latin)*

Which in English translated as:

' *The Shadows protect those that hide from light, though light brings sanctity from darkness. All those that shall fall under thine protection shall themselves be saved.*' *(English)*

Ms Pemberton spoke softly to the child, "Do not be afraid, we are here to help you, but I need to know who you are and if you remember how you got here?"

The child started to cry, tears falling from her eyes like soft rain. The small child tried to move from between the bodies surrounding and trapping her into the space. At every turn she dislodged an arm or flailing limb but inch by inch the girl moved closer to Ms Pemberton. Slowly she reached the spot where Ms Pemberton had wedged herself. Ms Pemberton reached forward and picked the child out of the mass of bodies. She sat her on her lap and looked at her closely. As they gazed into each other's eyes, tears welling in their eyes, it was as if Ms Pemberton knew this girl. You know, really knew her as if she were family or even her own child. But surely this could not be possible or probable because Ms Pemberton was not married nor did she have family in this area.

I now moved gradually to where they were huddled. Ms Pemberton was stroking the child's hair lovingly and cradling her close to her chest in a nurturing way, as a mother lovingly cradling her babe. I reached Ms Pemberton's side and stopped at her feet, leaning in towards her and the child. I quietly asked, "How do you know this child? Do you know who these people are?"

Ms Pemberton held my wrist and spoke gently and softly as the child slept in her arms. "Barney, this child is my little sister. She was lost many moons ago to this village and Frederick de Soames' curse."

Barney and Ms Pemberton looked on in disbelief. Were all these bodies people from the village's past?

I looked further down the passageway as the swells of undulating bodies rising from their slumber were coming to their senses. In the stillness each body started to sit upright, they all looked towards Ms Pemberton and I as if for an answer. Some were holding the talisman in their hand; they looked relatively unharmed if not a little dishevelled and dazed.

One man shouted, "Where the hell am I? This is not the right house."

Then one by one they screamed, shouted and wailed in unison, a cacophony of noise railing against us. The sound in Jasper's hallway pinned us to the spot, part fear and part sheer disbelief, for we had stumbled from one hell into another.

We moved slowly, the child clinging to Ms Pemberton. Time was racing past; we had to rapidly find answers. In the silence life itself seemed to stop.

"Barney, what should we do?" Ms Pemberton stopped suddenly and stared blankly at the sea of bodies strewn around us.

"Ms Pemberton, all we can do is move on, find the answers wherever we can."

Back to back now we surveyed everything. I closed my eyes as if to make a wish. I had to get out of the situation, or should I say, we all had to find answers. I needed to ask Ms Pemberton what had happened to the Major, the two soldiers, Harold Prestwick and Reginald Winterbottom.

"Barney, should we head to Jasper's cellar or find somewhere to sleep?"

I could hear the faint sound of someone calling from the depths of the cellar. An unease engulfed me, the voice sounded familiar yet impossible. For the voice I heard sounded like that of my grandmother, long since dead and buried. Something was happening here; it was as if time itself was unravelling before our very eyes. What was happening and why was I here in the epi-centre of this nightmare? Too tired now, eyes heavy with sleep, I stumbled through the pitch black and unrelenting sea of bodies down the steps and into the depths of the dank cellar. A presence pressed close but remained eerily silent. Crashing to the ground I lay on dusty feed sacks, now too dazed and exhausted and unable to fight the drag of sleep.

I drifted off past everything that surrounded me and into the reassuring safety of sleep. Ms Pemberton and the child rested against me as we huddled to keep each other warm. In my dreams I was far from this nightmare. Here it was as if life was as it had always been. I was still living in the Big Smoke, leading a great life, happy and completely carefree. Everything was as perfect and as grand as I had in reality wished it could be.

Was this real or a dream playing itself out bit by bit?

Oakley Place lay stripped bare, soulless and devoid of warmth. An empty shell of destruction immersed in blackness. Doors wide open like mouths aghast with fear, windows smashed, leaving shards of glass glittering on the ground, particles of hope left to decay in yesterday's stolen dreams. Just off the village green the curtains twitched, from one house to the next. Yet how could this be? Were these the dead of days gone by, reliving past memories or the ghosts of our future?

Ms Pemberton and the child she had named Celia were now deep in sleep. I lay restless in this filthy pit of despair, past the aching need for sleep and the fear of what was unfolding second by second. We were caught in a never-ending loop, time unravelling like an old well-worn jumper.

Barney paused and listened to every creak and crack that echoed around him. He wondered if his mother and father knew what this was all about. And now he realised why they had been so delighted when he had announced his plans to move to Oakley Place. The secrets of his family were now unfurling like a flag of doom. How was it that Ms Pemberton was his matching key in this whole story? What was the link and why here and now?

Suddenly there was a loud explosion, then heavy pounding footfall above his head. Dust dropping through the cracks in the floorboards above his head. He then heard the familiar voice of Frederick de Soames, and the screams of those who lay displaced above on Jasper's floor, as they were being rounded up like cattle.

Eyes riven shut with fear, as I pretended to be dead. An old tarpaulin shrouded all three bodies from the gaze of Frederick de Soames. We clung together like grapes on a vine, silently hoping that Frederick de Soames would leave Jasper's house soon.

Then all three, felt the chill of death graze their sides. Frederick de Soames moved slowly past them pausing at each step to scan the terrain.

Barney, Ms Pemberton and the child held their breath as they lay there in the opaqueness of the night, silently daring not to breathe in case it caught the attention of Frederick de Soames.

The child began to stir, Ms Pemberton holding her close to her chest. Frederick de Soames lingered at the place where they lay, the tarpaulin hanging over them unconvincingly. Frederick de Soames seemed to be suspicious and was keen to move the tarpaulin. He moved in towards them slowly. We lay frozen in fear, our eyes wide open looking on into the unfolding nightmare. Beads of sweat ran free along our brows, as we were trapped in a torrent of this never-ending circle of darkness.

Then there was silence.

Light started to flood the other side of the tarpaulin, daylight filtering through: casting-shifting shadows against the white wall. We watched hidden as Frederick de Soames and his men quickly departed. They seemed eager to escape the light of day; hurrying footsteps racing up the flagstone steps and echoing through the corridors above our heads. The three of us moved carefully and slowly from under the protection of the tarpaulin, strands of light enrobing us with the heat, as we began to thaw from the effects of icy fear.

Ms Pemberton stood and said, "Barney, what do you think that was all about? Why do you think Frederick de Soames stopped in his tracks like that?"

The sheer sense of joy in her voice was palpable.

Barney paused and took a deep breath. "Ms Pemberton, will you and the child wait here, please, until I give you the all clear? I'll go upstairs now to check that they have definitely gone. Something just does not feel right. Of course I could be very wrong, but there's just a stack of things that do not make sense as they tumble into place, and there are more than one or two things starting to stick out like sore thumbs."

Barney knelt down to examine the footprints that had been left by Frederick de Soames. "Can you see this slimy residue that has been left? It looks like slurry of some kind. Do you think he's been back to John Yarrow's farm? And if so, I wonder why? What do you think, Ms Pemberton?"

At this point Ms Pemberton was leaning against a stack of dusty boxes reading a packing label. She suddenly turned towards Barney, who was ascending the flagstone cellar steps. "Barney, do you think the secret is at John Yarrow's farm?"

Barney shouted down at her in the cellar, "It's a possibility, I suppose. Not sure why though, or even where we would start looking."

Barney was now at the top of the flagstone cellar steps, which led to the ground floor of Jasper's house. The bodies, which had previously littered the corridors and hallway, had vanished. Even more bizarrely, Jasper and Mrs Stanton were sitting having afternoon tea in the living room as if nothing had happened.

Jasper turned in his seat and looked up towards me, "Hello, Barney lad! Where have you been? We've been calling you for hours to find out if you and Ms Pemberton and your little one want to stay here while they're repairing your place."

Barney stood stunned into silence. He looked around the room. Everything was clean and shiny; there was a faint smell of lavender wafting on the breeze. Jasper and Mrs Stanton looked less dishevelled than last time. In fact they looked smarter, younger, rejuvenated.

"Jasper, what has happened? I'm confused. When I last saw you and Mrs Stanton you were both in a wretched state, and to be honest I did not think either of you were going to make it."

Jasper stood up quite spritely for a man of his aging years. He then put his arms out and pulled Barney towards him embracing him tenderly as if he were his long-lost son.

"Jasper, what are you doing?"

Barney felt uncomfortable with this sudden show of affection; it was not as if they were family or that close.

Jasper looked Barney squarely in the eyes and said, "Barney, what's wrong? After all, we are family, aren't we? Especially now you and Ms Pemberton are together, that is."

Barney tried to move away but was caught in Jasper's full embrace. Pushing backwards he managed to loosen Jasper's grip and fell awkwardly backwards, landing heavily in a large armchair. Barney sat crumpled and perplexed, not sure what was going to happen next. He could hear the excited footsteps of the child racing up the flagstone steps and the dutiful footsteps of Ms Pemberton lightly brushing each stair with a graceful footstep.

Mrs Stanton was busily preparing the table, setting a place for us all as if it were the norm. Her dress now reminiscent of the 1940s era and, come to think of it, so was Jasper's attire. As I looked through the window I could see children happily playing on the village green, while across the way the village shop seemed lively, with people toing and froing gleefully. The sun was blazing down, and all was serene and blissful.

Then Jasper said those words that still ring clear in my head to this very day.

"Barney son, why has it taken you so long to return to me and your mother? I understand the nightmares, especially those about the future that seem to plague you like some vile disease. Nothing's changed though, son. Me and your mother still love you, son."

Jasper moved forward again, as if to once more embrace me. I felt a pull in my stomach, like an invisible cord was drawing me in towards him again. Then a pelt of sickness rose in my throat, before consuming my body. Breaking away rapidly, I ran to the bathroom along the corridor, a short distance from the living room. I grappled with the door handle and dived through the door, slamming it hard behind me. My hands landed heavily on the rim of the sink bowl, as I leaned in and out retching, and trying to erase Jasper's words, which danced proudly in my head.

I then looked up suddenly and caught a quick glimpse of myself in the mirror above the sink. Only the image staring back at me was not me. I looked around behind me, in case someone had entered the room without me noticing. There was no one there but me. Just me… and the stranger in the mirror. This person staring back at me from the mirror looked older, more self-assured. I didn't recognize him, as he looked like a 1940s spiv, with a thin moustache and greased back hair. I moved backwards and forwards towards the mirror, just in case it was some weird illusion. Moving back and forth, like some crazed lunatic unsure of his own shadow.

In the stillness, with thoughts drumming in his head, Barney slumped down onto the toilet, his head in his hands. He pondered once again on what was now unfolding once again before him.

*'What if I was not who I thought I was? What if I have slipped back through time? What if this was all some ridiculous dream? I wondered if I could shrug this off. Was it possible that I was slowly*

*going mad?'*

As he sat motionless and unclear on his route, he heard heavy pounding outside the door.

"Barney, are you all right in there? You've been in there for hours. Come on love, we've got to get home with Alice before the blackout."

*' It was Ms Pemberton all right, on the other side of the door. But what was she talking about and who was Alice? The little girl in the cellar had said she was called Celia.'*

I waited before making my move towards the door, trying to give myself time to think carefully before speaking. Well, after all, something was most definitely not right here, as I had suspected. Only nothing looked so dangerously wrong, either.

I rushed towards the door, and pressed my head against the flaking brown paintwork. "Ms Pemberton, is that truly you? Say it's really you. What was it you said just now? Say it again, please say it again but slowly as you're not making much sense."

Ms Pemberton drew herself up on her tiptoes, pressed herself hard towards the door and shouted through the cracks, "Barney, we've got to get Alice home before the blackout. Will you damn well stop all this tomfoolery,

Barney! What has got into you today? Treating your mum and dad like that after all they've done for us and all that."

She stopped mid spiel as if she had been interrupted by something.

"Ms Pemberton, are you still out there?"

Barney paused and waited in the eerie silence.

"Ms Pemberton, are you still there on the other side of this door? Please say you are there."

# Chapter Seven
# The Missing

In the stillness my breath was thick as it condensed on the mirror. The temperature had plummeted, ice weaving out along the walls and window like a frosty web.

I grabbed the damp towel from the rail and wrapped its dampness around me, hoping to gather some latent heat. My skin was now starting to feel rubbery and icy cold. The reflection staring back at me, from the other side of the mirror was pale and wane. I feebly called out, hopeful for a response from Ms Pemberton.

From the other side of the door came a faint sound. The slowing beat of a heart, ebbing and flowing at each pulsation.

A rasping voice spoke, fragmented, "Barney Lumsden, your time's running out. It's time to give yourself up; after all, you can't run against time forever. You're running out of road fast! Best stop running now while you can."

Barney, too tired and weak, gripped the fragile wood of the door.

"Who's there? What do you mean? What is happening?"

Barney now lay pressed against the door, crumpled and frozen.

On the other side of the door stood John Yarrow, frail but wily, with a steely glare in his eyes.

Mrs Stanton, Jasper, Ms Pemberton and Alice were gone!

No longer even the merest essence of a presence, not even a whisper on the breeze; back once more to the present.

John Yarrow slowly ambled around Jasper's home. He foraged through cupboards and boxes to find an implement to enable him to prise open the bathroom door. He knew that Barney was running out of time fast. John Yarrow also knew that had it not been for the heroic efforts of Barney that day, calling the police and finding him in his farmhouse, who knows how the situation would be right here and now.

"Barney lad, hang in there, don't give up just yet. This story ain't over, we need to get back to how things should be but only you can do that, only you, Barney."

The village was just as it was when Barney had found John Yarrow. But now by some bizarre twist of fate, their roles had been skewed and reversed. Here was Barney smashed and splintered now looking for a rescue from the one he had rescued.

John Yarrow looked frantically for anything, just something he could use to lever open the door. Barney's luck was almost out; the rapid race to release Barney pressed too close for comfort. John Yarrow rummaged through boxes, hopeful of finding some implement that would prise open the door again after several fruitless attempts. Now down to the last dusty battered box, he tore off the lid, like one of those crazed mobs of Frederick de Soames. John Yarrow's movements seemed to be on an unending loop, repeating and repeating like a record stuck in its groove. Time seemed to be circling, pulling out wide like a giant vortex, while dragging them in against their will, drawing and sucking them in at each pressing moment into its core. Was this the eye of the storm, or was this time unravelling loop on loop? How could this motion be stilted?

Silence hung heavy around John Yarrow's frail frame.

He was unsure of his stark choices.

Standing looking deep into the abyss he hoped above hope that he and Barney could make it out of there in one piece.

It surely could not be that impossible? After all, they only had to pull together, find Jasper's car again and drive off into the sunset. If only it was as simple as that. If it was that blatantly easy, why hadn't Barney and John Yarrow legged it long ago? Hours raced away like a rushing river, washing away hope as rapidly as they clung tight.

In the stillness, with hopes evaporating, we waited. Barney lay motionless against the brittle door. He sensed something light was growing like a blanket, pulling him closer and drawing him in. A being stood at the centre of the light now as he was slowly being joined by other figures. As each one moved in closer their faces became clearer as though they were ghosts of the past. The centre figure of the swelling mass bent down, reached forward and scooped me up holding me close.

Was this the end?

Was it all over, the final chapter of my life?

The light being emitted escaped through cracks of the door. John Yarrow was on the other side of the door, he'd stopped – frozen to the spot. He watched as the door bulged in and out as if it were breathing.

The pressure built behind the door; it swelled and then exploded, fracturing and splintering in to razor-sharp shards, each fragment spiralling up and out into the clinging air. John Yarrow dived and hit the floor at speed before being showered with jaggered splinters of wooded sinews. Like an apparition looming in some strange ether, the beings moved forward. Barney was being held now as if being cradled like a babe in its mother's arms.

The hallway of Jasper's house was illuminated in the strange swirling white light. The air was filled with the voices of many, resonating the with joyous song of a million angels.

Barney slumped, delirious, his heartbeat quickening and fading. John Yarrow was stunned into silence as the room enrobed them in its eerie whiteness.

In the stillness, life seemed to stop. Nothing stirred until a heavy odour filled the room; the air was being sucked out, as the strange aroma permeated the space. The smell of death pressed close, as if the Grim Reaper were standing ready with his scythe. John Yarrow, now exhausted and shattered, knelt down to Barney who had been in the process of squeezing through the panel that John Yarrow had smashed through the door. Barney was half in and half out of the door, before it had fragmented.

The front door swung on its hinges, like a sail on a ship cast out by a raging sea. As the door swung it cast strange shadows of figures, lurking unseen, hidden in the darkness and out of view. They moved like slowing waves of drifting corn. Silently and relentlessly moving, slowly ebbing like rolling tides of blackness.

John Yarrow pulled his jacket taut around him and held Barney firmly. Barney, still lifeless, his body a heavy pendulous weight upon John Yarrow's frail shoulders, pulled him from his point of centre.

"Barney, can you hear me? Not far now and we'll be out of here soon and off to better days."

Barney raised his head as if he had heard every word John had uttered. Then reaching the door they clung close, moving hastily towards the partially open door. John sensed a presence, a familiar smell. The smell of wooded amber hung strong and fragrant like that of his beautiful and beloved Penny. There were other smells too, all distant reminders of his past. Each one anointing and filling his senses. With Barney's head resting hard against his shoulder. A breeze drifted and lifted the young leaves from the trees and gently and effortlessly tossed them down. Barney seemed to be regaining his normal self at each painful step. He was not fully in the here and now, of his present moment. Not fully awake and filled with the summer of life. Barney was now a frail figure of his formative youth. No longer carefree and boyish in his ways. Lost in the moment temporarily, scrabbling to get back to reality.

Clinging on tight to John Yarrow, Barney slowly pieced together bit by bit like a gathering curtain. Now at the edge of moving forward, and as close to the door as they could be, a sudden breeze caught the door agape, and smashed it back towards them. The heaviness of the door swinging forcefully back towards them momentarily floored them.

Regaining his composure and determination to succeed, John ran with full force, Barney welded to him like a limpet as they dived through the front door of Jasper's house into the light of the day. The brightness of the daylight engulfed them and held onto them in its loving warmth and bright array.

Outside, the air seemed to hold some essence of revival; Barney took a large gulp of air. Then reacting and scrabbling back up, he caught his breath.

John sat crumpled on the ground, absorbing the aftermath and examining his options, while planning his next move. He felt tired and wondered how he could make his forward progress, particularly with Barney in his current state of play.

Moving slowly, he had also realised that he was not fully recovered from the ordeal and terror of the farmhouse fiasco. The tiredness trapped him and his only wish was to sleep. He lay down in the long grass on the village green amongst the daisies, which laced the carpet of grass. Barney slumped with his eyes closed up against the old oak tree, its branches broad and wide.

The day was bright and the fragrance of summer filled the air. Birds flew darting to and fro, carefree and without concern for John and Barney.

All was silent, little sign or sight of anyone milling about on the village green that day. The doors of the old village store stood wide open, the sign at the entrance flipped lazily as the breeze nudged it repeatedly.

Dozing now, both lost in slumber, no cares for Frederick de Soames or what was or had been. Those times were irrelevant for now they were just themselves. At each passing minute life sprang forth, growing as an emerging and changing picture being drawn sharply into view.

Barney and John seemed to be out for the count for hours. Everything around them was rapidly changing as if they were caught in some kind of time vortex. Sleep kept them in a state of stasis, unchanged and unchanging.

Like a jigsaw the pieces were starting to fall into place. What were they to do next? Would their gentle slumber provide them with an answer? The questions were never-ending and endless, as they lay littered around them like empty soulless words – strewn freely.

The houses around the village green, now became alive and vibrant: people moving busily in and out, to and fro, cars whizzing by, horns sounding to alert wandering chickens, curtains now springing back into life, twitching and flickering out a code from one place to the next.

As this growing activity increased, Barney and John slept on, each fragment of life breathing in and out, reinvigorating their weary lungs, forcing out the stilted stale air. Life demanding them to breathe: to cling strong to life, to wake to the vibrancy of the day.

John Yarrow tossed and thrashed at the grass around him as if fighting unseen demons. Barney had wedged himself within the protruding roots and was nestled like a child. Minutes raced to hours, not pausing for change or silent sleep.

Children played now on the village green, curious about John and Barney, unsure of these strange beings and why they were there.

Sleep enveloped, them pressing them closer to secrets untold. Barney and John silently ebbed and flowed, all life drifting closer to the finite of drawing death.

Yet life was eager to continue its journey: watching as a mother gently cares for her children. Each sound rolling towards them, like waves crashing in and rolling out. The children lost in joy growing and expanding in radiant hope for a new future in Oakley Place. More trusting and hopeful for truth and a new reality.

The light around them grew ever brighter. Silence bustled with vibrant calls of joy. Everything started to awaken, including Barney and John. From their deep night of slumber, the vista before them cleared to reveal their own time. Both of them seemed now to be aged, worn and changed. The reality was also now dawning on them, that time had been erased. What had been their past was now becoming their present.

In the distance they could see figures drifting into view. The etheric visitors seemed to grow and press closer to Barney and John Yarrow. Visions or illusions of Ms Pemberton and Silvia Yarrow? Then voices spoke from vacant frames.

Dust swirled, creating a haze of uncertainty.

"John, this makes no sense. How can they be here, when they are not here anymore? I just want things to return to normal, to how they were before."

"Barney, we just have to accept this and discover what we are being taught. Life is indeed full of mystery. Your role has not been completed, it seems."

Barney got to his feet, brushing down his hair and straightening his worn clothes. Ms Pemberton and Silvia Yarrow stood in a haze – they were both trying to speak. Their mouths were moving, but it was as if the sound had been – turned down – muted by time itself. They flickered, fragmented images as if projected – yet chillingly realistic.

It was all getting too crazy.

John Yarrow now peered beyond the visions.

Something had caught his eye in the distance. On the other side of the village green there were clouds of smoke emanating from the direction of where his farm used to be. Before them now grew another vision, but this time they were standing in front of a blazing farmhouse, flames shooting from the windows, which melted like rivers of molten glass cascading down. But was it an illusion or had they slipped through another portal in time?

John Yarrow stood silent and stunned by the vision in front of him.

"Barney, why is this happening again? I cannot take much more of this madness. Please, when will this stop? Can we just go back to how things were?"

"John, I think there is something missing – this is not real. Look, can you see? There is your prizewinning herd. Well—"

Barney stopped abruptly.

He couldn't tell John Yarrow that he had seen his prizewinning cattle trussed up and dripping in blood.

"Barney, what made you stop? Is there something you're not telling me? You are hiding something. Please tell me what you know, it's not too late – what do we need to do, Barney? Just tell me – I just cannot go on with this never-ending nightmare."

John slumped to the ground, crumpled and drained of life, the sense of impending doom unravelling, moving fast and shifting like desert sands. The roar of fire rattled through the crumbling building – the echoes bashing their ears, deafening them and driving them back.

Barney plunged his hand into his pocket, pulling out the talisman. Suddenly, as if by magic, the vista of the burning farmhouse was erased. They were back on the village green – Silvia Yarrow and Ms Pemberton were sitting with them as if it was a normal Sunday afternoon with friends in the summer haze.

We laughed and chatted about what our plans for the future would be. Ms Pemberton sat close and gazed lovingly. It was as if love was sweet upon our breath. Children's laughter lifting and rising through the rustling leaves. Optimism and hope glistening on the breeze. Ms Pemberton's talisman gracing her slender neck, the words lay against her skin.

I leaned in towards her and whispered, "Is this real? What's next in this journey? Tell me more about the talisman. Do you know what is next?"

Moving closer Ms Pemberton spoke softly, "Barney, this is as real as it can be, for now that is – somehow. There are rumours that Frederick de Soames and his kind are still lurking. We also have to find Alice and the others – they're still here, lost somewhere."

Far into the distance something drifted slowly – a curtain flickered, and then two or three more joined in the melée. However, this time was different from the many occasions before – I glimpsed one of the Twitchers. Although not visibly clear, I was certain that something was amiss. The figure appeared to be covered in open sores – could they have been simply communicating their imminent demise? Something was definitely not right – according to the story Ms Pemberton and the Major had spun, and indeed led me to believe.

I also wondered what exactly had happened to all those tortured souls back at the lab. The antidote was now all but used up. Surely they should have been thinking about leaving as soon as they could, right? This journey was slowly turning this boy into a man.

For a brief moment he thought about his parents, the lies and tall tales he had created in order to escape the city, the hellish nightmare of family life, as he had known it. His dad had been a city analyst, and his mum a top PA – both passed by each other's lives like ships in the night. There had been little time to grow up and ask questions, like most of his mates had.

Barney Lumsden was wise and astute beyond his years.

He had, had to be that way in order to survive.

# Chapter Eight
# The Street

At fourteen he had run away – his parents had paid little attention and although they had looked for him for all but a week, their loss was a mere interruption to their own busy lives.

Barney had lived out on the streets, drifting from doorway to doorway and from one drama to the next. After three years of living in cardboard boxes under dank, rat-infested bridges and doorways, he knew it was now time to move on with his journey.

On one such day, he had been lying in an old crypt sheltering from the elements, when he came across an old book and an ancient talisman. Without giving it much thought and having to make a sudden dash out of the crypt, he had bundled everything into his holdall with a possible view to selling them, to make some cash.

Then one fateful day he had been rummaging in bins at the back of some old Government office buildings looking for scraps of food. Feeling so hungry, he came across a little more than he had bargained for. From out of the shadows someone came up behind him.

"What you doing, lad? They're secret – now hand 'em back or I'll blow this whistle and before you know it the Bill will be all over this place like a rash on a nipper with the pox."

Barney turned and came face-to-face with an elderly security guard – the name badge on his uniform said 'Jasper'. Barney quickly backed away, hurriedly stashing the document and dropping the remnants of one of the takeaway boxes on the floor, while throwing the contents of the second one in his holdall.

Their eyes met, curious and quizzical as if they had met before. It was if they knew each other, like a grandparent and his young charge. Could it have been the case, or was Barney just delusional from the cold and hunger?

"Yeah, well, old man what ya' gonna do then? Go on, go on then, blow your whistle – get the rozzers on me. See if I care. Doubt they'd catch me anyway."

Jasper span sharply round to catch hold of Barney. He missed, but knew a few tricks and tried again. This time he managed to knock Barney to the ground. Barney hit the ground at full force – the old man not realising his strength. But then Barney was weakened and a mere lightweight in comparison.

Jasper knelt down to Barney, "Sorry about that, lad, but you had it coming to you. What are you doing around here anyway?" Jasper was now perched on the edge of a step, bending down towards Barney. "A young kid like you should be home – not out here – come on lad, where do your folks live? I'll radio in and get someone to contact them and come and get you. This is no place for a kid like you."

Barney raised his arm, "You crazy old fool! Why did you do that? And well, as for calling my folks – you must be joking! As if they'd care."

Jasper was engorged with rage, "What are you trying to say? Where are they? Any decent parent wouldn't let their kid just disappear and fend for themselves – would they?"

Barney looked away – staring into the distance and gathering himself – the pain sat upon him raw, and bleeding the colour from his face.

"You would think not, but my folks don't seem to think that way."

Jasper felt crushed, as if he had been run over by a speeding train.

"So where are you sleeping tonight, lad?"

Barney paused.

He didn't want to appear needy or fall prey to the old man's pity. "Jasper – right, that's your name, old man – right? Well, I'm going to go back to join the others under London Bridge."

Jasper stood to his feet, trying to block any exit where Barney may try to cut a dash from the place. "What do you mean, lad? But you're a kid – you shouldn't be out on these rat-infested streets so late at night. Wait here, I'm going to speak to my better half. See if we can put you up for a few nights at least, until I can figure out what to do, that is."

But while Jasper was securing the area and making a call home, Barney had legged it – gone like a flash of blinding light. Barney was now running, panting for breath and trying to block the thoughts racing through his head. What if the old bloke had been genuine, not some weirdo like so many times before? His determination to get away from Jasper had pushed him forward to the point of being on the home straight to London Bridge and the hovel with the other homeless. He could see a few folk milling about ahead of him. Not far now and he'd be back, safe and unknown once again. Some of the others there had lit small fires, embers burning the gathered cast-offs of the day-trippers and visitors who had been roaming earlier in the day. You'd be amazed at what you can come across in bins. He reached into his holdall and rummaged about, pulling out the stale Chinese carton. The contents of the carton were rank, the smell made him retch. Well, this was supper and it was either that or another night of nothingness. Barney wondered if Jasper had really wanted to help him. After all, it had to happen, I suppose, sooner or later, didn't it?

He was greeted by the one they called 'Scary Mary' – I had tried to speak to her before to ask her why she had ended up in this place – but I always ended up being on the end of her ranting's and verbal abuse. The first time I met 'Scary Mary' had been some while back. I had been sitting minding my own business when she came and plonked herself down next to me. I remember how she turned with her face almost pressed to mine and started ranting at me, her face filled with so much anger and hate it was palpable.

She was going on about David Cameron and how he needed to be castrated – all those with money, then turning with a mocking look at me, insinuating that I was the same. I tried to calm her down as it was quite clear something had triggered her off again. I felt concerned about the young homeless mother who was trying to get her two young kids off to sleep – they must have only been about five and eight years old at the most. 'Scary Mary' turned to me in a rage and said, "Why do you keep saying okay? It's not okay."

I shuffled uncomfortably, trying to extricate myself from where I was sat. I hadn't meant to be condescending or thoughtless; I merely wanted to shut her up so the poor kids could get some sleep. I plucked up the courage and asked her to move – I just had to get away from her seeping anger and negativity before it started to bore into my skin. I managed to find somewhere else to sit not far from the young mum cradling her kids to keep them warm. 'Scary Mary' was now fast asleep, hopefully dreaming of something nice – at least that's the very least I could hope for her and, come to think about it, for any of us here under this dank dark bridge on the coldest night on record.

How had all these people come to this?

Why was I here in this damn mess too?

It really made no sense whatsoever!

As I leaned back into the railings I reminisced about times with my folks, the holidays to far-off places, the expensive presents they bought me as a child, the times we laughed. We laughed a lot when I was young and I really thought my mum and dad loved me too…well, that's how life was back then. Until everything changed. They both seemed to gain this lust for life; mum with expensive tastes and dad with his penchant for fast cars. It all cost money and as they had seemed to want more, they started to change. That's when I started to be less important to them. They stopped laughing and the love just seemed to run out … Well, that's enough wallowing for now.

It was now 4:30 a.m.

Sleep was brief and it was time for us to disappear. The commuters would be moving along soon enough, tut-tutting and looking down their noses as they passed us by.

I've got to find my way back to that Government building and see what else I can find out, May be there'll be other useful stuff, who knows. I thought I may have just caught the old security bloke, as I scrambled over the fence.

But instead I was immediately met by a flashlight.

The voice shouted, "WHO'S THAT? COME OUT AND SHOW YOURSELF."

Barney hid in the shadows.

The voice shouted again, "I SAID, WHO IS THERE? COME OUT OR I'LL SHOOT."

Jasper was changing out of his uniform and putting on his old familiar clothes. Not many days now until retirement, then he'd be able to enjoy life. No more commutes into London. He was looking forward to late mornings, long walks in the countryside and escaping the Smoke for good.

Jasper and his lifelong partner, who he called Mrs Stanton, lived in Oakley Place, a tiny little corner of heaven in the heart of the Buckinghamshire countryside.

# Chapter Nine
# A New Home

As Jasper was counting the days on the calendar he noticed a figure stumbling and dodging the flashlight from the office window below. He stopped counting the days to freedom and was now pressed up against the windowpane watching intently to see who was out there lurking in the dusky shadows. He caught a glimpse of a tatty old holdall – he remembered that the kid from the previous night had had one exactly like that. It couldn't be him again, could it?

Jasper dropped what he was doing and ran down the stairs – he knew that he had to be light on his feet, whilst hedging Barney off and away from the flashlight. Trying to avoid the smashed broken glass, and the splinters of glistening shards, Jasper edged closer to the skittering shadow as it dodged the beam of the flashlight – the shadow ran and was now running out of cover.

Jasper whispered, "Is that you, Barney lad? It's me, Jasper, remember from the other night? What are you doing here again?"

Barney stopped.

There was now nowhere to run or hide anymore. It was either stop, or listen to what he had to say or be caught – he was too tired, cold and exhausted. From the shadows he said, "Yeah, old timer, it's me all right. Can you get me out of here before this trigger-happy fool blasts me into outer space?"

Jasper squared in front of Barney, flashed his light and gestured him to stop and be quiet. Jasper then shouted, "Frank is that you mate? It's Jasper here. I have just come out to get some fresh air – Stan's been on the baked beans again and well, it stinks to high heaven in that office. It nearly took my breath away, all right."

Jasper and Frank walked back into the security hut. Barney moved near the gate just as Jasper had gestured, and waited.

Inside, Jasper grabbed a can of coke and a couple of slices of bread, a bit of cheese and a handful of Bourbon biscuits. He hoped these would keep the kid going until they got back to his home.

He shouted, "Night, Frank. I'm off now – see you tomorrow. I hope you don't get too much hassle tonight."

From the security hut Frank called after Jasper, "Night, Jasper. Be sure to say hello to your missus for me – 'night!"

At that Jasper left and darted to where Barney was waiting. Jasper hurriedly moved them away from the gate and found somewhere out of reach to speak to Barney.

"Barney lad, what were you thinking, coming back like that? Do you have some kind of death wish?"

Jasper reached into his bag and pulled out the food he had gathered and the can of Coke and handed them to Barney. "I got these for you to keep you going until I got you back home."

Barney stopped, "What do you mean, home? I didn't agree to any such thing."

Jasper stopped, shocked, "I thought you would want the chance to start again, a new beginning, a new life. Well, the other half and I would like you to come and live with us. It's out in the sticks but at least it's away from London. The room is comfortable and you'd be free to do as you please. Just say yes, you have nothing to lose, Barney. If it doesn't work out, you can come straight back to London and join your friends back on the street again. No harm done, hey Barney? What do you say?"

Barney sat, looking confused.

He now had the opportunity at last to have people around him that really cared about him, that may in time love him too. Who knows, they may even understand him a bit?

Thinking, Barney examined the contents of his holdall, checked out his worn shoes, looked at his hands heavily layered with ground-in dirt, then quickly looked back into the eyes of the kind old stranger. What really had he got to lose? A new chance, one that he'd been waiting for, for so long, no more 'Scary Mary', no more rifling through bins eating remnants of other people's leftovers.

This thought lingered in his head, and danced on his tongue like the delight of a juicy hamburger washed down with a Coke. After some serious soul-searching Barney could not do anything but accept Jasper's invitation.

Getting to his feet and brushing away the grime of the smoke, Barney said, "Okay, old timer, you got me – I would be absolutely bonkers not to accept your generous offer. However, I want you to know that I am my own person, I don't want you treating me like I'm your kid – now you won't, will you, Jasper? I'm done with being bossed about by grown-ups and although I am grateful to be leaving this nightmare, I have managed so far without grown-ups telling me what to do, and if you've got any funny ideas about sending me back to school, you can just forget it. I hope you understand, Jasper."

Jasper smiled and nodded, "Whatever you say, Barney. We'll just be a bolthole; there'll be a bed to sleep in, food in your stomach and we'll be there for you if you need guidance along the way. I promise we'll not interfere. So what do you say, Barney? Shall we give it a go?"

Barney and Jasper shook hands and headed off towards the train station. A new road had begun for them both, and neither knew where it would take them but for now it was an exhilarating journey into the unknown. An adventure: into trust and who knows.

# Chapter Ten
# An Alternate Reality

The past and my future whirled around before me that day on the village green. I had seen so much darkness, so many unclear thoughts, even when it was painfully there, real as life before me. I had to find the missing piece to this puzzle - the answer may have been within me but how would I ever know?

There had been Twitchers in London, watching my every move from the tall shadows they had cast across my life from the day I had been born to the moment I was spat out by my parents. Here and now once again I was being taunted by these beings shrouded in mystery, the Twitchers this time in Oakley Place. I had to find the secret, and crack and decode this ancient code. What was I missing and why was Ms Pemberton hell-bent that I held the key to solving and ending the nightmare? She seemed to think I was the key and the only one to close the portal and dissolve the past.

The day withered into night, its hues of colour washed by the blackness of the encroaching night. We all parted company. I went back to Jasper's house – the door swung on its hinges – no trace of what had happened before. Normality had resumed somehow and it was once again as it had been when I arrived in Oakley Place. Jasper sat in his favourite chair near the open fire and Mrs Stanton was busily filling the house with glorious smells of cooking.

I headed up to my room at the top of the house, dived through the door and landed on the bed. As I lay there pondering life, the Universe and everything I had discussed with Ms Pemberton that afternoon, something new started to become clear. Sitting bolt upright I cast my eyes towards the top of the old dresser. It was piled high with dusty books and old decaying newspapers. I then remembered the documents I had gathered from the bins that night at the old Government building, and then more followed. Where had I put the talisman and the old book I had found in the crypt? Could they possibly hold the answers?

Feeling slightly delirious and heavy with the expectation of a breakthrough, I started shifting through the papers and books on the dresser, tossing clouds of dust up into the air. I gasped and choked on the settling dust.

I fumbled through the books at speed and wrestled with the pages of the one I thought I had found in the crypt. It was an old book of Jasper's on the art of living an alternate life. It seemed the old man was hiding a secret too. I carried on looking; I was now determined to find the book, it had to be there somewhere. I had also come across a map and a set of co-ordinates. It was an old map of Oakley Place. On further inspection it also looked like there were some underground tunnels and an old ancient burial site. I stopped looking for the book for the moment. I was now curious – my eyes were transfixed on the map. Stealing my eyes, away I now noticed the papers I had gathered at the old Government building that night.

I put them all together, held them to my chest and hoped that maybe, just maybe, I was nearer to finding an answer. Hopeful that I was reaching a turning point, and climbing that mystical hill. I quickly laid all of the papers out across the floor, some draped over the bed – well, who needed sleep anyway? I had plenty of time to sleep another night - tonight I had to start to stitch the pieces together. It was time to create the life I wanted, which had so far been out of reach. Now it was speeding like an out-of-control locomotive rattling down a one-way track — heading straight for my mind.

In order to try and keep my sanity in this never-ending vortex crunching nightmare, I had delved into alternate worlds and had been reading some books by Mike Dooley, a leading teacher and manifester in the realms of the Universe. I had also watched a film called '*The Secret*', which completely blew my mind. I wondered if there was some kind of link with everything I had seen and read. I did believe that we made our own realities through our hearts and emotions, and that thoughts created things.

Barney sat on the floor of his room, the colours of hope swirled, creating a rainbow of light across the white wall in his room. For once, the shadows peeled back, letting the remnants of the day through. He held his head in his hands. Could he be that close, really close? If he just hoped and thought with all his might, maybe with a whipping wind the mystery would be revealed. Barney sat, his eyes closed in deep thought, locked off from the present, the here and now.

# Chapter Eleven
# The Dawning

As dawn penetrated through the worn curtains shielding Barney from the world, shards of piercing daylight caused pinpoints of stardust to pepper the walls with a white iridescence, waking a slumbering fully clothed Barney from his crumpled heap on the bedroom floor.

Whipping the sleep away I was back in the here and now once again, and ready now more than I had ever been, to tackle this hill rising up in front of me. It was now 5:30 a.m. and I could hear Jasper snoring and Mrs Stanton muttering in her sleep.

I heard the birds waking and greeting the morning like a long-awaited mistress. There was a clatter outside in the street below and then I heard the screech of cats yowling and fighting amongst the bins.

Rapidly preceded by a bullet of air, which rushed through the open window as if something had shifted, the trees on the village green swayed as if being lifted by an unseen current. A roar of swirling wind had started to build, wave on wave like a growing tidal wave of chaos in the street below. Bins were being blown over, clattering and smashing against fence posts, which seemed to totter like deranged ballet dancers on buckled heels before splaying out into a sea of broken limbs and debris. It was now about 6:45 a.m. and the weather was changing minute by minute and time was eroding second-upon-second. It was as if time itself had fractured disintegrated across all portals of space and beyond.

The weather outside and the sudden rush of air through the window had distracted me from the evolving picture being created around my feet. Then, as if night had followed day, the storm gently retreated, ushering calmness.

Jasper was now prowling up and down the landing as if he had been searching for something.

I poked my head out of the bedroom door, "Jasper, are you okay? What are you looking for out here on the landing exactly?"

He seemed to be in a trance of some kind and totally oblivious to Barney's presence. Hitting the light switch caused Jasper to bolt as if he'd been startled. Jasper blinked in the brightness of the light, his pyjamas worn and baggy, drooping down and dragging as he walked.

"What you doing up so early, Barney?"

Turning around, Barney saw the book he had been looking for all night poking out from underneath a pile of packing, which had been buried deep beneath layers of rubbish on the landing. It was a mixture of Barney's stuff and that of Jasper and Mrs Stanton's, an ever-growing mound of yesterday's forgotten treasures.

Mrs Stanton was now out on the landing too, bleary-eyed and wrinkled in her nightdress and an old dressing gown that was wrapped around her frail form.

"What is all the commotion going on out here on the landing, Jasper?"

Mrs Stanton couldn't quite hear Jasper's response; she had become a little hard of hearing of late.

"Go back to bed. I was just looking for that book. You know, the one Barney has been asking me about."

Jasper stopped in his tracks as if mesmerised by something glinting just out of clear sight. Mrs Stanton hobbled along the passageway towards Jasper. She was still totally oblivious to Barney. She too was now mesmerised by something glinting in the daylight. Barney moved forward, trying to see what they were looking at so intently.

"Good morning, Mrs Stanton! Good morning, Jasper! Is everything okay? What are you both looking at so intently? It's almost as if you've both hit the jackpot or found some long-lost treasure. What are you both staring at?"

Silence filled the passageway. All three now stood as if in a trance of some kind. Standing there transfixed by this strange mist forming before us — what was happening? Then, as strangely as it had appeared, the mist dissipated and was gone as quickly as it had arrived. Jasper and Mrs Stanton stopped what they had been doing and returned to their bedroom, banging the door hard behind them as if shutting out a secret.

I was baffled. Had they not realised what had just happened? Turning back into my own bedroom, I noticed something glinting on my bed — I accidently kicked through the once carefully lain papers strewn across the floor, sending them skyward across the room — all my hard work undone in a flash of mad exuberance to get the talisman, all hope undone in a blinding flash for the sake of a quick fix and the realisation that it had something to do with the talisman. Hold that thought for just a moment. Could I really have found the answer to all of this? But how could the talisman be the big answer, the solution? It couldn't be that simple, could it really?

Barney stood looking out through the window, one hand pressed upon the glass and the other holding aloft the talisman, which shone, causing glimmers of light to fracture each strand, casting a strange pattern across the wall.

In a daydream and without realising, Barney quickly glanced once more at the talisman before stuffing it hurriedly in his jeans pocket. He looked around the mess in his room and, without thinking, gathered all the pages back together and placed them on the dusty dresser. Barney looked out of the window and noticed a few familiar faces. Passing the mirror he fixed his hair, checked himself out and left the room.

"Bye, Mrs Stanton, Jasper. I'm off out, I'll see you later," rushing down the flight of stairs he cornered into the hallway and bolted towards the front door.

Jasper shouted down, but it was too late.

I was unsure what had happened earlier that morning, as exited through the front door. It felt as if something had changed and may be not for the good or bad of this unfolding situation.

# Chapter Twelve
# Finding Answers

On the village green, Barney had met up with Ms Pemberton who had been joined by Harold and Reginald. Wow! The old gang back together but how could that have happened? They found somewhere to sit and chat. Bizarrely, Harold, Reginald and Ms Pemberton had no idea whatsoever what Barney was going on about.

"So where have you two been hiding the last few days? You wouldn't believe what's been going on here – you've missed it all!"

Barney looked baffled.

Harold, Reginald and Ms Pemberton looked at each other then leaned in towards Barney saying as if in unison, "Barney, did you have the talisman with you or had you left it behind again? And what's all this nonsense about curtains, Twitchers and this character, Frederick de Soames? That's just some ancient mumbo jumbo that was in that book you showed us all on the day you arrived. Don't you remember? We all spent ages leafing through the pages. It had a few incantations that we tried out but nothing happened at all – total phooey if you ask me."

Barney stood up abruptly, casting his gaze out across the village green and quickly looking around the houses to see if the curtains were moving. All curtains were still, not a flicker or a Twitcher in sight.

Ms Pemberton stood and joined him, "Barney, what is all this about? You seem confused. Is it something Mrs Stanton has cooked you? I know some of her creations can be, well, just a little bit interesting, shall we say. You don't think maybe you've got a touch of food poisoning that's been making you hallucinate? Something similar happened to me too a while back. It took me a few days to get myself back on my feet. You'll be okay, I'm sure. Well, Barney, I'm sorry but I've got to go and meet Martin Fothergill, he's got some news – I'm hoping that he's finally come to his senses."

Barney gasped and stood back staring at Ms Pemberton.

"Sorry?! Say that again, Ms Pemberton."

Ms Pemberton was now picking up her bags and starting to head off towards Leverstone Manor.

"Wait, Ms Pemberton!"

Barney ran at full pelt, leaving Harold and Reginald looking on agog but not thinking anything more about it and scribbling down their plans for the day ahead. Barney caught up with Ms Pemberton, grabbing her arm as she was about to exit the gate on the village green to swiftly make her escape. She stopped, spinning towards Barney, she seemed different not so young and carefree. A little dishevelled, and motherly looking – a reminder of his mum he had left behind so long ago.

"What is it now, Barney? I did say I had to go and, well, my time is precious." She brushed Barney's hand and arm away as if swatting a fly.

Barney in his panic begged her to stay.

"Okay, you have five minutes – you had better make it quick otherwise Martin Fothergill will have my guts for garters."

Barney had not heard that statement since he was a little kid; it had been something his own mum and grandma used to say to him all the time.

"Well, Ms Pemberton, it's just you said that you're going to see Martin Fothergill. You see he's dead, isn't he? We left him at the laboratory. You were there - and the Major. Remember? We all got suited up in protective gear before we came back to the village. Do you not remember?"

Ms Pemberton's calm demeanour was passing and had grown into an angry glare. Staring at Barney her eyes seeming to pierce his gaze, "Barney, I really do not have time for this nonsense, you are being absolutely ridiculous. My goodness, you've certainly got a fantastic imagination. It's a shame you're wasting it by making up such damaging rubbish. I'm going, Barney. Maybe we'll speak when you have come to your senses."

Barney felt as if he had been punched in the stomach by the one person he could talk to, with whom he had shared so much. He fumbled in his jeans pocket and pulled out the talisman, holding it in the air as a skittering Ms Pemberton busily dashed along the High Street towards Leverstone Manor. Feeling sick and crippled with confusion Barney stood rooted to the spot. Was this all real or had he been making this all up? Why was this happening? Maybe his parents had been right; maybe leaving home, maybe 'Scary Mary' and all her tall stories about things unseen had taken hold and buried itself deep within his skin.

*'Okay, I'm going to ask Harold and Reginald. They're sure to remember the farmhouse, aren't they?'*

Harold sat upright against the old oak tree; he'd somehow wedged his posterior into the roots. "It's quite comfy here in this little hollow. Woo hoo, Barney Lumsden chatting up the local talent, eh? You do know she's, well, you know, having a fling with Martin Fothergill, don't you. Wouldn't like to be you if he finds out!"

Barney looked at Harold, "What are you talking about? I'm not having a fling with her. We've been trying to find an answer to this!" He pulled the talisman from his pocket again.

This time it was met with stunned silence. Harold and Reginald seemed to be backing away.

Harold stumbled, his words garbled, "Barney, what the hell are you doing? Put that damn thing away. Hide it quick, even better let's bury it where no one will find it."

Barney now looked at the talisman. No, nothing looked any different. Reginald was also now quite animated and was moving towards the bench.

"Reginald, what's wrong, mate? Stop being so weird. What's wrong with you two? Oh, I suppose what I've said is all a load of baloney just like Ms Pemberton seems to think it is all just a figment of my fertile imagination. Furtive! Imagination – Pah!"

Restless and uncomfortable, Harold was shifting himself, re-adjusting his composure and trying to act as if Barney was just going off on an unhinged ramble.

"Barney, me old mate, maybe you need to go and get some sleep. Put the talisman away and best forget about your contretemps with Ms Pemberton. I'm sure she'll be all over you again soon like a rash—those types always come round, right Reginald, isn't that so?"

"So where have you two been for the last few days?"

Barney was watching their expressions trying to gauge just some clue. Anything would have been better than nothing at that moment in time.

"As we said, Barney mate, we think that it may be prudent if you were to go back indoors and get some sleep. You said yourself that you'd been up all night sorting through some papers and looking for the stupid book. Didn't I tell you to ditch it that day after we'd been leafing through the musty pages of that old book?"

Barney couldn't gauge his response; it was if they were skirting around something. It was now starting to become very clear that he was not going to discover any answers from either of them.

Why were they being so downright defensive in their responses? What were they hiding? What was the big secret, the answer?

# Chapter Thirteen
# The Twitchers' Code

Barney was back now within the confines of his bedroom. He could hear Harold and Reginald yapping on the village green, below his partially opened window, which seemed to offer hope. Perched on the edge of his bed he listened intently to see if he could garner any clues or resolve a myriad of unanswered questions.

Getting up and moving towards the dresser and the pile of papers he had left discarded in his haste that morning, Barney now noticed his old tatty holdall and, better still, the book he had been looking for. There, now larger than life and incumbent shedding of answers in amongst all the papers, or maybe there'd be something written about who or what the Twitchers were. Barney gathered up all of the papers and the book and sat on his bed.

Slowly strolling through each page, devouring every word to sate my hunger, I sifted and hoped I'd find just something, anything. There it was in black and white within the first few pages of the book. I read on with interest, curious to decipher fragments of a code. The page in the book headed ' **Twitchers** ' read as follows:

*' Twitchers: These beings are the gatekeepers to the nether world. They hold the keys to the gateway. They remain unnamed though through time there have been many. Some have walked beyond you, unmasked and yet still not awake. They are protected by time itself, though ancient beings they do not age nor are they aged by time. Time is but an illusion, a delusion of mind; a facet of man's fragmentation of paradoxical time and space. Reality is but an imaginative foray into an open vortex of the unseen.*

*The Twitchers are the masters of the code; this is the password and key to unlock all meaning.*

*They shall protect those who walk in the now and prevent their demise.*

*At their first arrival they crafted a talisman, which they imbued with magical qualities, it is said that the talisman would protect the wearer but may unhinge the portal in time if the secret words written upon the talisman were read and unworded.'*

Barney stopped.

' *Unworded* ', what was that supposed to mean? He didn't even think there was such a word.

His head ached, question after question knocking on his tired brain and fading his splintered mind. Tiredness seemed to grab him by the throat, and force him back into a fretful sleep. The book lay open at his side, as the breeze flipped the pages.

A presence was now also watching over the slumbering Barney Lumsden.

*You see, I had been waiting, just waiting, for Barney to read these words now for so long. I hoped he understood and realised. The answers were here or maybe they were not. I have been watching and will continue to watch until he solves the code. He is doing remarkably well, don't you think?*

Barney moved in his sleep, tossing and turning almost as if he were fighting some hidden dragons or demons. As he moved he dislodged the book, sending it crashing to the floor.

*That was my cue to leave, depart again and wait quietly behind my curtain, beating out my warning to him, hoping he would understand. You see, I had been a Twitcher for millennia, here at the time of the plague in Oakley, as it was back then before they had added the 'Place'. Back then when the plague arrived we had such a bad time with the clergy. Shall we just say they were a dying breed?*

*Barney was still deep in sleep, the book falling to the floor had not even dented his dream state. Amazingly Jasper and Mrs Stanton had not rushed in to see either.*

*I decided to wait a while longer to try and illuminate you, the reader, to see if you would possibly help shed light for Barney when he awakes.*

*The vicars of Oakley, and the village, had almost been decimated by the plague back in 1349, you see, most of the houses had rats, dirty beasts covered in fleas. When they popped their clogs and shuffled off their little mortal coils, the fleas would jump off and nip the humans, thus passing on the bubonic plague or Black Death as it's now purported to be called. There was no escape from the place, those who had managed to survive hid in the tunnels underneath the old manor house. A few of us stayed in the village trying to warn off folks passing through. We decided to make a talisman and used the skills passed on by the Wise Ones. The first talisman we had crafted seemed to have no effect; though we had tried as hard as we could we were not able to protect the visitors. The folk who seemed to have been born here and who had been given a talisman seemed to make a good recovery. As if by magic one or two seemed to be revived and plucked from death's door as his scythe had been coming down ready to take its final blow.*

*Death, after all, was only an illusion — a season of change in everyone's unending journey. I'm certain Barney will find the answer and close the gateway.*

Back in 1349 is when Frederick de Soames had arrived in the village, a traveller from far-off lands who many seemed to think had somehow transported the rats carrying the plague. He tried to learn what we had been doing and interfere; he knew more than he should so we had no other choice.

A few folk had turned back to the Wise Ones for answers, some felt protected by the herbs and concoctions that appeared to ease the ailments of the plague. Frederick de Soames was the one who started all the issues with folks being tried as witches. At some point he had managed to get out of the village unseen and alerted a local witch finder. That said, every Wise One's days were numbered. Frederick de Soames blended into the background as if transparent yet watching, always watching for his chance to spread blackness.

So one night in the depths of despair, the Wise Ones of Oakley gathered and lured Frederick de Soames into a trap, one which he had been intrinsic in setting and had attracted the eyes of the witch finder himself.

I and one or two others followed Frederick de Soames to the edge of the woods, which surrounded the village. He was waiting to pass information to a local witch finder. We hid and watched. He was dressed in his finery looking like a landed member of the community. The witch finder arrived and they drank mead together and then there was an exchange of papers. One of the people with me stepped back, crunching a broken stick under foot, sending parliaments of rooks ascending and a cacophony of sound echoing through the wooded *boughs of the trees. Frederick de Soames and the witch finder hastily parted company and went their separate ways.*

*We followed Frederick de Soames back to his lair and it was there that we laid him low in the un-consecrated ground. This was to be our downfall as he was indeed the blackest of all souls. As we fought to take his last breath, he cursed us with all his might, his words venomous and deathly — we seemed to be surrounded by shrivelling blackness as if trapped in a never-ending terror. The two with me were spat out like arrows. I stayed and stood my ground; I would not let this nighthawk go nor let his blackness steal what we had been trying to protect. I had wound one of the talismans around my wrist and hand, and with my blade I plunged it into his heart hoping to pierce the blackness in his soul.*

*There was for a moment a violent wind which ravaged the trees around me and the blackness lifted. At my feet lay Frederick de Soames in his dying minutes and through his mutterings he had said, "Death shall be my steal. I will remain forever blighted to this place that you have ripped me from, my soul cannot be claimed. Thee shall suffer and I shall remain until death is mine."*

*I moved the earth, rubbing the stain of blood and death into the ground. Using broken branches I crafted a casket over his body, then making fire with two sticks rubbed together I set the mound ablaze. No one in the village would have suspected anything was amiss. The fire raged on into the early light of dawn, casting shadows of figures lurking in the blackness of night turning into day.*

# Chapter Fourteen
# The Twitchers

The Twitchers stood behind their respective curtains like sentry guards, although no one was ever sure why and what noble deity they were guarding so determinedly. Hidden from view and cloaked in anguish and despair. For these poor souls had been cast out by society, and were destined to watch and warn all those who had not been born and bred in Oakley Place.

Twitchers were in many ways kindred spirits with the Wise Ones, who had also been lost in the vortices of time and space, their existence an unending loop of lifetimes, rolling on and on, unceasing. These unfortunate souls had been afflicted by the aftermath of the plague. They lived in half-state lives between two planes of existence. The Wise Ones, namely Jasper and Mrs Stanton, had nursed these beings through the death throes of the plague.

A deal had been made between Frederick de Soames and the leader of Oakley back in the 1340s that all those with no bloodline would be destined to walk between two planes of existence, the seen and the unseen, until the demise of Frederick de Soames. On that night when Frederick de Soames had been murdered in the woods, and his body had been laid low in un-consecrated earth, and his bones were burned to ashes, the curse was not broken; it was thought that there would be no sanctity for these beings.

Jasper and Mrs Stanton had been charged by the village elders to care for the Twitchers, to protect them and shield them until someone returned to bring release to their souls and free them from Frederick de Soames' curse forever.

Jasper looked distressed; his heart was racing and his words raced from his lips like a colliding passenger train. Mrs Stanton held his arm as Jasper tried to continue speaking to Barney, Alice and Ms Pemberton.

"You see, Barney, Alice, and Ms Pemberton, we had also had a child that is, myself and Sarah Seagrove around about 1348, a short year before the plague had arrived. Lovely little thing she was, bonny and bright as a button. One late summer afternoon, shortly after Frederick de Soames' arrival in Oakley Place, our little lamb Martha lay in her crib. Sarah was worried as she did not seem to want to drink or feed. There were no doctors at that time. We both searched our books of potions and treatments, and consulted the ancient oracles and ways. But we could find nothing. Martha grew weaker day by day, and by then the plague was bringing death to all quarters of Oakley Place. On one early morn, Sarah went in from the garden where she had been collecting herbs from the meadow. I was in the coppice clearing and preparing graves for the dead, and trying to stay away from those in darkness of the plague. I heard a scream and wailing and hurried back to the hut in the woods where we lived. Sarah was cradling our darling child within her arms against her chest. There was no life within her frail sweet bones. Sarah would not leave the child, not even in death. We found some consecrated ground where plague victims had not been buried and held a burial for our precious child."

Jasper and Mrs Stanton sat with tears rolling down their faces.

Alice, Barney and Ms Pemberton looked on, moved with emotion but unsure if Jasper and Mrs Stanton were acting out a drama or reliving something from a book. It just seemed too unreal for words. Had they both been taking something? Maybe they were simply hallucinating or maybe Jasper and Mrs Stanton had eaten something that had started to cause some chemical imbalance in their brains.

Barney leaned in towards Jasper. "Is everything okay? You and Mrs Stanton don't seem your usual selves. Did all that stuff you just told us all really happen – only we were just wondering if you were making it up?"

Jasper looked furious and sprang to his feet, "Barney Lumsden, after all the things Mrs Stanton and I have been telling you and trying to explain to you over the months, has not even one bit of that sunk into that crazy head of yours? Barney, I truly despair."

Jasper and Mrs Stanton left the room angry and offended by Barney's questions and lack of respect. Crying, Mrs Stanton grabbed Jasper's arm to steady herself, "Jasper, I thought Barney couldn't be so cruel. I thought he understood about all of this."

Jasper attempted to calm Mrs Stanton and they both went into the living room, closing the door firmly behind them.

Barney sat in the parlour with Alice and Ms Pemberton.

"Whoops! Don't think that went down very well. I'm just getting so sick and tired of all the weirdness: Wise Ones, Twitchers, and Frederick de Soames. What else is likely to appear, the Four Horsemen of the Apocalypse? It seems we've all offended Jasper and Mrs Stanton because we don't believe them both and think they're making it all up."

Ms Pemberton and Alice both sat with their eyes glazed over.

Ms Pemberton said, "Barney, I think you need to be a bit more understanding; this is not like you one bit. Everything that Jasper and Mrs Stanton have told you about is the truth. They're the most decent people in Oakley Place. I think you need to maybe go out for a walk to think about how to put this right with them both. After all, Barney, who knows where you would be if Jasper and Mrs Stanton hadn't rescued you from living on the streets."

Barney sat.

It was now time for him to listen and learn.

"Ms Pemberton, so the Wise Ones, the Twitchers, Jasper and Mrs Stanton, it's all real?"

Ms Pemberton leaned back in her chair, staring at Barney.

"Yes, Barney. Yes, it's all real. As real as you are sitting there: and me here. The Twitchers are here but we're all being watched by unseen eyes. I should know that, working for the Government."

Barney sat feeling uncomfortable; he was trying to digest Ms Pemberton's last statement.

*What did she mean, the Government and what was the link to do with the Twitchers?'*

The mind boggled.

He looked at Ms Pemberton, "Let's go and get that fresh air. I'll apologise to Jasper and Mrs Stanton when I get back. I also want to see what I can find out about the Curtain Twitchers of Oakley Place."

Barney and Ms Pemberton left the parlour and drew back the heavy front door. They glanced behind them to see if Jasper or Mrs Stanton had ventured out from the living room. The living room door was still firmly closed.

Alice had now come back in from the garden and had decided to join Barney and Ms Pemberton on their walk around Oakley Place.

"Barney, did you sort it all out then with Jasper and Mrs Stanton? I heard Mrs Stanton, she sounded devastated. I think you're going to have to eat a lot of humble pie to get back into her good books. Wouldn't like to be in your shoes, Barney, trying to wiggle out of this conundrum. I just don't get you sometimes, Barney. What do you think, Ms Pemberton? What do you think is going to happen?"

Ms Pemberton and Barney hovered in the doorway, half in, half out, in mid-progress of their exit.

"Alice, I think that Barney needs to do the right thing and say sorry and tell them both how much he is really grateful for everything they have both done for him. Hopefully Jasper and Mrs Stanton will forgive him. After all, they seem to love him like he was their own son."

Barney hadn't been quite prepared for either Alice or Ms Pemberton's statements.

"Well, I suppose you're both right. I did deserve Jasper's outburst in a way. I didn't really mean to upset or offend either of them; that was never my intention. I'm just so freaked out by all of this stuff. I thought I had got away from it all when I left London and especially after leaving 'Scary Mary' and all her wacky stories . . ."

They could all hear footsteps in the living room, as if someone was nearing the door. Barney looked at Alice and Ms Pemberton, "Well, I think that's our cue to go for our walk. I'll tell you more about 'Scary Mary' as we walk around Oakley Place."

All three now left Jasper and Mrs Stanton's house, closing the heavy door behind them. As they walked towards the village green Barney started to continue his story about 'Scary Mary'.

"Scary Mary was the resident doom-monger in our little hovel. She was a bit like a mother hen type, completely off her trolley. But it takes all sorts, I suppose, and sometimes she would say half decent statements if you were lucky.

There was one day when she'd suddenly gone off on one of her major rants. Yes, I remember really clearly now. She said something about being watched by the Government and that we're all watched from the moment we've popped out of our mothers until the day we die. 'You can't see them though,' she would say. 'But mark my word, lad, they're always there, those filth bags they are, them that's stole my house from me and put me out on the street to fester like a wild dog.' Sorry, I didn't mean to come across so aggressive it was as if I was right back there again. I think I may stop there."

Barney seemed visibly shaken. Alice and Ms Pemberton stood looking at Barney, their mouths agog.

"Barney, are you okay? You seem a bit agitated."

Barney was trying to calm down and regain his composure.

"Yes, I'm fine. I still find talking about all of that business on the street too hard. Every time I do, I feel as if I'm right back there as real as this place."

A curtain twitched at one of the windows on the green.

"Ms Pemberton, Alice, did you see that? Look there's another. What do you reckon is going on now?"

Back at Jasper and Mrs Stanton's house across from where the three were standing on the village green, Jasper and

Mrs Stanton were starting to calm down and take stock of everything that had been said. Clearing his throat and smiling at Mrs Stanton, Jasper repositioned himself, "So Sarah, what do you think we ought to do about the lad? It just wouldn't be right to boot him out the door and send him packing, would it? He's had more than his fair share of all of that. I think it's all just got a bit too much for him maybe. Shall we give him a second chance? After all, you know we'd both miss him if he wasn't here."

Mrs Stanton had stopped crying and had calmed down.

"Jasper, I am really unsure what to do with Barney. Maybe we need to get the Twitchers to help him to understand. That may work. What do you think, Jasper?"

Jasper looked alarmed at the mere prospect of Barney meeting the Twitchers face-to-face.

"I think we need to find a way to get Barney to understand everything. Yes, we need to find a way that the Twitchers can somehow speak to Barney without him actually seeing them as they are."

Mrs Stanton and Jasper took down a large weighty book, which was covered in strange writing across the books cover. Some of the symbols were almost like those that Alice and Barney had been looking at in the book that Barney had.

Barney, Alice and Ms Pemberton were walking back down the High Street towards the village green. They'd been walking around the whole village chatting and talking about life, and general chitchat about Jasper and Mrs Stanton, and the Twitchers. All three of them were now almost back at the place they had started from on the village green.

A shadowy figure left Jasper and Mrs Stanton's house and darted back to one of the houses on the village green. Barney, Alice and Ms Pemberton just looked. None of them spoke; they just looked. Had they just seen one of the Twitchers and if so, why had it been with Jasper and Mrs Stanton?

# Chapter Fifteen

## Sleep

Night and day had somehow merged – Barney slept for days, or so it had seemed. Mrs Stanton, Jasper and the doctor stood by his bedside. It was complicated, was all that was being said. The book and papers had disappeared. On the dresser now stood a vase of spring flowers, which had been arranged with love. A card mingled within the leaves and petals read, 'Get well soon – we've got a job to do'. The name had been scrubbed out like a dirty stain.

His youth lay before him.

"How long has he been in this state?" doctor Saunders asked Jasper and a tearful Mrs Stanton.

Jasper, bending down towards Barney to cover him up like a young child, replied, "It's difficult to say really. You see, he's not our kid. I found him living on the street in

London and, well, it broke my heart and when I spoke to Mrs Stanton – well, that was it really, we knew all right – the boy needed a home, some grown-up support. No idea where his family are, he wouldn't say anything about them – it all seemed too much for him to bear. I tried to ask many times, but he'd just clam up. We felt it too cruel to keep on asking so we never did."

Doctor Saunders peered at Jasper and Mrs Stanton in disbelief. He said, "Wait, so you have a young adult living here that you know nothing about him, no history? That's tantamount to kidnapping, isn't it?"

Jasper shuffled towards the bedroom door, nervous and alarmed at what the doctor may do next. As he edged closer Jasper said, "Well, not really. You see, we were doing him a favour – taking him off the street like that."

The doctor was now starting to punch a number into his mobile phone. Hastily, Mrs Stanton left the bedroom, saying that she had to attend to something in the kitchen.

Jasper put his hand on the doctor's shoulder, "Well, I think that's it for today. Thank you very much for popping by."

Jasper bustled the doctor out of Barney's room and closed the door behind him. As they approached the stairs the two men's eyes met, no words spoken just a stilted silence – there was no need for words really, was there?

Doctor Saunders said, "You do know I'll have to notify the authorities, don't you, Jasper, and we'll need to find his parents. Barney is a very sick young man."

They were now at the foot of the stairs. Jasper had turned towards the doctor and was moving him towards a partially open front door. Now, leaning forward, Jasper widened the opening, bringing the door fully open. He looked out into the street saying, "Thanks for coming by, doctor Saunders. Feel free to pop back soon to check on Barney – I'll phone his parents and let them know. I'm sure they'll be by to pick him up – bye then and thank you once again."

Jasper had of course no intention of calling Barney's parents – even if he had known their whereabouts. Doctor Saunders had not completed his call, and in the hurry and bustle of being bundled out through the front door, he had forgotten that he needed to make urgent calls to the authorities. From the door, Jasper watched as the doctor strolled down the road towards his car, attentively watching and eager for the doctor to drive off and leave Oakley Place once and for all. A few curtains around the village green seemed to twitch and flicker.

Coming back into the warmth of his home and the admiration of the dutiful Mrs Stanton, Jasper ambled into the living room and sat down in his favourite chair near the open fire.

Looking at Mrs Stanton, he whispered, "Well, that's him gone – I bet he'll be back again soon. We need to get Barney back on his feet ourselves, Mrs Stanton. Let's see how he is tomorrow, then we'll start to set him straight."

Mrs Stanton nodded nervously, she seemed overwhelmingly concerned and spoke softly back to Jasper, "So, Jasper, what are we to do if the doctor comes back? What will happen if he brings the police? We'll be arrested for kidnapping. I'm too old now to be lumbered with a criminal record or a conviction."

Changing the subject Jasper laughed heartily and replied, "Well, I don't think that's likely to happen. Shall we go into the parlour, my love, and have a nice cup of tea and some of your delicious homemade scones with fresh strawberry jam?"

Upstairs, Barney thrashed about, the blankets winding around his sodden body, at each turn they wound around him like a straitjacket, pinning him to the bed and making him a captive of sleep. Memories of life on the street evading his fractured mind and eating into his worn soul.

Lying in this dark place, a silent void, cold, hollow and black. In his dream state Barney saw his life like a book, each chapter his journey so far. The book had no ending but was it he who would have the final say?

Down below in the parlour Mrs Stanton and Jasper were making merry and appeared to have no cares in the world; the door was partially ajar. As they sat in each other's embrace they reflected and discussed their next steps. Jasper had also said that he thought it time to board up the cellar again. He also said that he'd need to go down and just get rid of a few things and do some tidying up. After that they'd be able to board the cellar up again.

Their pleasant blissfulness was disturbed by a knocking at the front door. Hurrying to their feet and rearranging their clothes, Jasper slowly moved towards the front door. Mrs Stanton stood cowering in case the inevitable had quickly arrived. Jasper turned the lock and slowly edged the door open to see who was on the other side. He could see a female jittering to and fro in desperation. Now feeling a little less fearful he opened the door a little wider to engage with the female standing near to the door.

"Yes, can I help you, young Miss?"

The young woman, turned towards Jasper and Mrs Stanton, who was now standing by his side.

"Hello, I don't suppose I could see a Barney Lumsden, could I? We have something we need to discuss. It's really urgent that I speak to him right now. Where is he? Is he here? Sorry, I should probably say who I am."

Jasper and Mrs Stanton stepped back into the hallway, beckoning the young female.

"Why do you need to see Barney in such a hurry? What has he been and done now? That boy is always up to something, we never know where he's been or what he's been up to. Mrs Stanton, I bet he's let this poor girl down. That Barney, told you we need to set him straight – leading young lasses astray and all that now too."

The young woman's eyes flitted back and forth between Jasper and Mrs Stanton as she watched each word they spoke.

"So, where is Barney? It is rather urgent that I speak to him. I cannot wait too much longer. You see, time's running out."

The young woman seemed fretful and panicked as she frantically paced back and forth, her footsteps drawing lines across the tired parquet floor.

"Yes, I think I remember – Jasper, that's your name, isn't it, and Mrs Stanton?"

Jasper and Mrs Stanton looked at each other perplexed and puzzled. Who was she and how did she know their names? There was a loud thud above their heads and a muffled groan. Rushing past the young woman, Jasper and Mrs Stanton ran upstairs to see what had caused the noise. The two had now been duly followed by the young woman.

Then she made her unannounced entrance through the doorway of Barney's bedroom. Barney was hanging in stasis from the tangle of bedclothes. The young woman rushed over and started to try to untangle Barney from the mess he was in. One of the sheets had wound tight around his neck and had they not stormed in, he may not have been so lucky. Barney rolled back on to the bed, the colour in his pale cheeks returning, like the rose of a china doll. His eyes fighting against the pulled-down shutters, desperately trying to open and see who his rescuer had been this time.

The young woman stood in the doorway, the light creating a halo and adding to her almost angelic appearance. Maybe he had passed to the other side and was now on the brink of freedom – his own personal Nirvana.

The young woman introduced herself: "I'm Alice, I've just got back and, well, I have a message for Barney. We need to do something urgently and only Barney can do it. Do you know where Ms Pemberton lives? I need to visit her too. You see, they both hold separate parts of the key."

She paused, watching a waking Barney Lumsden. She leaned against the doorframe and put her head back, as if trying to gain some Divine intervention.

Jasper and Mrs Stanton were now pacing around the room, wringing their hands and watching – breathless at each second.

Like a butterfly breaking from the encasement of its cocoon, Barney was reviving painfully slowly. They agreed that they would all wait, and wait all night if they had to.

# Chapter Sixteen
# The Reawakening

The dawn arrived flooding, the room with light and waking all within. Barney awoke and lay looking around the room, checking to see if anything had changed. He breathed out to see if he could see his breath in the cold air. Curled on the old chaise longue at the far side of the room was Mrs Stanton, and propped close by her side sat in a crumpled heap, a dishevelled Jasper. At his bedside, leaning with her back to him but propped against the bed, sat a young woman with blonde hair. She smelled of cherry blossom, and was rested against the bed in deep sleep. They all looked so peaceful in their dream states.

Barney glanced around the room; he was looking once more for the book and the papers.

"Where have I been? I feel as if I've been asleep forever. Mrs Stanton, Jasper, you awake? Lady, who are you and what are you doing here in my room?"

He was met with a stony silence, the air in the room seemed to plummet and the mist reappeared – a figure now standing beckoning to Barney.

Barney reached forward to try to touch the figure, "Who are you and what do you want? Why do you wish me to follow you?"

Looking around the room, I thought whatever this being wanted would be short and the others – the young woman, Jasper and Mrs Stanton were all fast asleep anyway and wouldn't wake. Slowly rising from the bed, he moved towards the figure and reached in towards the widening vortex now forming amidst the mist. Now in the midst of the vortex Barney followed. He didn't think this was death. His room was now no longer there; he was now sitting in a grand hall.

The figure opened a book, which looked similar to the one he had found in the old crypt in London. I explained to Barney as I had the day before he had drifted in to this dark night, that he was the only answer to unlock the code and stop the return of Frederick de Soames. I told him once again that he had to decipher the code and pointed to what he had to do in the book – it was all there in front of him; he just had to read and understand.

Barney scoffed and laughed, "You are joking, aren't you? You must think I've fallen out of a tree and landed on my head. Okay, so that may be partially true. But I do not understand what this writing is; I've never seen anything quite like it. It looks Latin or Arabic, it could even be Sanskrit."

The figure pointed at the words again, trying to emphasise each word. There were now other beings gathering, all trying to add their interpretation.

Barney stood to his feet waving his arms, "Okay, okay, that's enough! I can't hear myself think in here."

At that moment it was as if something popped, the sensation jolted Barney to his senses. He was now back on his bed, Mrs Stanton was awake, as were Jasper and the young woman.

"Oh my goodness, Barney lad, we're so glad to see you awake."

Jasper now perched next to him on the bed trying to hug him, quickly followed by a crying Mrs Stanton blubbering all over Barney. In the shadows stood Alice, trying not to spoil the moment of this happy reunion.

"Hi Barney, I've come to help if you'll let me?"

Barney looked towards the figure dipping in and out of the shadow.

"Sorry, I can't see you. Who is it?"

Alice now stepped forward and moved closer. Barney looked up and met her face. Their eyes locked like missiles, searching to find what each other wanted to say. Jasper and Mrs Stanton sensed that it may have been a good time to leave, but also wanted to make sure that Barney was truly okay.

Jasper patted Barney on the back and said, "Barney, are you okay if Mrs Stanton and I just go and get some air? I don't know about you being asleep for a month – I feel as if we've been asleep for a century. Best let you find out what this young lass needs, she's been by your side all night. Whatever she needs to talk to you about must be pretty serious stuff. Come on, Mrs Stanton, let's leave Barney and young Alice to have their chat. I'll come back soon, Barney, with a drink and some food. I bet you're feeling parched and as if you could eat for King and Country."

Barney was still locked onto Alice and lost in thought. Alice moved closer, sitting next to Barney on his bed.

"Barney, do you remember me? Do you know where Ms Pemberton is too?"

Barney was confused. He knew who Alice was, but before she was a young child and here she was now almost the same age as him.

"Barney, I came to help you and Ms Pemberton put the pieces together. I have some clues and some answers."

Alice, now excited and very animated, pulled a notebook from her satchel, which had been slung across her body. She was busily etching words across the white cloudlike pages of the book.

"Alice, I don't understand. How can this be? Where have you been?" Barney's brow was heavy once again, steeped in grinding thoughts.

"Do you remember that day Jasper and Mrs Stanton were in the parlour and we were all having tea? You went to the bathroom and, well, you didn't ever come back. There was a loud explosion outside and we all ran to find shelter wherever we could. It was a bomb that had exploded near John Yarrow's farm. We thought you'd left Jasper's house as well. But we couldn't find you anywhere. We searched for weeks, visiting all the hospitals locally and even travelling to London. I then just seemed to get caught up in a group of people one day in the Underground in

London. I lost you both and ended up with a family. I promised that I'd come back to help you and Ms Pemberton and so here I am."

Barney sat stunned, his eyes glazed in disbelief. Was he truly awake or was he looping circle on circle, life on life? Giving him the slip and running him to the brink of madness. He pondered if that had been the fate of 'Scary Mary', and if that was how she had ended up on the street in the state that she was in. Alice was in full flow, drawing diagrams and writing frantically.

The door of Barney's bedroom glided open and Jasper came trundling in with a tray laden with two mugs of tea, some of Mrs Stanton's rock cakes and some dainty sandwiches, resting on perfectly white lacy doilies.

"Here you go, Barney. I said I'd bring some food to keep you going. How are you both getting on? So, how do you know each other?"

Alice was just about to speak when Barney said briskly, "Oh, we used to go to school together. It seems that Alice has just moved nearby and spoken to someone at the village shop who directed her here. We've got loads to catch up on. Thanks, Jasper, for being so thoughtful and bringing this food up – pass my thanks to Mrs Stanton too."

Alice was chomping her way through the delights on the tray.

"Well, Jasper, I don't mean to be rude but we really have got a lot to catch up on. Would you mind if Alice stays over tonight in the spare room?"

Jasper hesitated, "Are you sure, Barney? You seem to be tired still and, well, the doc did say…"

Barney was now looking at the writing in Alice's book and seemed to have been drawn into the page.

"I'm going now, Barney lad. I'm sure that will be fine about Alice staying over if that's what you want. I'll ask Mrs Stanton to do some extra food if Alice is staying and get her to make up the spare room as it's not been used in years. Sorry to disturb you both – enjoy your lunch."

Jasper shuffled, dejected, from the room.

"So, Alice, tell me again – I'm awake now and I need to know just what it is you need to tell me so urgently?"

# Chapter Seventeen
# Code Breaker

Down on the village green there seemed to be a building swell of people gathering. The noise of angry chatter rising on plumes of hot air, which filtered through the partially open window of Barney's room. Barney and Alice stopped mid-sentence.

"It's got to be something to do with them, hasn't it?" which was immediately followed by "What's his name? He's living just over there someone said, apparently it's all down to him." Just two of the ramblings they had managed to understand. Several people were now joining in the throng, sending the conversation in a million and one directions.

Alice squirmed in her spot – feeling a surge of gnawing terror take hold.

"Barney, do you think they're talking about us? That is, you and Ms Pemberton? What do you think is going on?"

Alice glanced out of the window, shielded by the curtain. She spotted at least three or four curtains flickering and twitching around the village green.

"Barney, I see what you mean about there being something weird about the curtains, and judging by what's going on outside we may have a few visitors soon. Is there a back door here or another way out just in case we need to make a quick exit? Judging by the tone they all seem to be quite angry about something. Phew! That was a close call; one of them just looked up."

Barney had now found the papers and the book – he was also scanning his eyes across the diagrams and notes in Alice's book.

"Alice, looking at this map this house is right over the roof of one of the underground tunnels. Let's go and look around downstairs to see if we can find any clues – I bet it's going to be really obvious – most likely right there in front of our faces."

They gathered all of the papers, the old map, the book and the two talismans; Barney grabbed an old army rucksack covered in camouflage and threw everything inside. Barney and Alice then made a rapid descent downstairs, almost knocking Mrs Stanton off her feet.

"Sorry about that, Mrs Stanton. I'm not sure if we'll be around for tea, but could you save us something for supper, please?"

Mrs Stanton tutted under her breath, "Barney, do you really think you should be racing about like this so soon?"

From the parlour came the dulcet tones of Jasper, "Mrs Stanton, is that Barney down to join us all?"

Barney stopped and looked at Mrs Stanton puzzled. What did he mean, join us all? Who else was in the parlour? Curious to see who was with Jasper, yet also caught on the horns of the unknown, Barney drifted towards the edge of the door. He did not want to fully commit but at the same time he needed to know who was there. Alice had wandered in to the kitchen and was unaware of what was unfolding.

"Barney, wow! I'm so looking forward to tea. Mrs Stanton is amazing, you should see all the things she's been cook—ing."

She stopped mid-flow, her mouth redundant of words and her eyes wide like plates. Barney was now trying to back away but with every step back it was if something or someone was drawing him back into the parlour. Alice hovered in the hallway, looking frantically and plotting their swiftest escape route. She could also hear a scuffle of feet outside the front door, as if something was about to burst through. Unsure whether to be bold and follow Barney into the parlour or now dive down into the open cellar door, Alice jiggled with uncertainty. The parlour was now very quiet; the chatter had ceased.

"Barney, is everything okay in there? It seems to have gone a bit quiet and we may have a few extra people soon. Shall we re-evaluate our plans, get the ball rolling, if you know what I mean?"

A baseball rolled out into the hallway and stopped abruptly at Alice's feet. She bent down and carefully picked it up, there was something written on one side in the funny lettering and then looking around the ball, Alice spotted a tiny slit with a slip of paper protruding.

Alice stood mystified, "Hey, Barney, what are you up to in there, and what's with the ball? You do know I was only joking about the ball – are you having some kind of a laugh?"

There was no response.

The hammering on the door grew louder, and the pounding seemed to shake the door from its frame. At the rate they were going there wouldn't be a front door soon. Alice decided it was now or never – what would be would be – she had no choice but to be bold, right?

Dashing forward into the parlour, a wave of thoughts and feelings rushed through her like a high-speed train about to derail. The rush pulsating and propelling her forward into the unknown. Alice stepped into the parlour — there was no one there. The room was empty, not even a sign that anyone had been in there for some time. Looking around the room, knocking on the walls to check if there may have been a hidden door, Alice then hurriedly exited the room.

"Mrs Stanton, do you know who was in there with Barney and Jasper?"

Standing by the front door as if she was about to open the door, Mrs Stanton stood primed and ready for whatever was on the other side. She had not heard what Alice had said moments before.

Alice tried to grab her attention, even if for just a few minutes. "Mrs Stanton, I don't suppose you have any idea where Barney and Jasper are, do you? Do you know who was in there with them – any idea at all?"

"What on earth are you talking about, girl? They're still in there. I can see them from here as clear as day. Jasper, Barney and a couple of Government-type folks. It's something to do with some papers that Barney found when he lived in London or something like that, I think. I'm not one hundred per cent sure though, I could be wrong. It's my age, I never get too fussed really. Well, I am nearly eighty-nine. I think my mind plays tricks sometimes, you know. A bit crazy, isn't it all really?"

Alice glanced back into the parlour. There was Barney, Jasper and two official looking people all gazing at the Government papers that were spread across the table. Standing at a distance Alice observed everything. Someone then moved towards the door as if they had sensed someone on the other side and did not want whatever was being discussed to spill out. The banging on the door seemed to peter out to a faint tapping. Alice spoke again to Mrs Stanton, who was now moving slowly away from the front door.

"Mrs Stanton, is there a tunnel or a secret passageway in the parlour or anywhere in the house, come to think of it really?"

Mrs Stanton pointed to the cellar and gestured to Alice to go down. Putting the baseball and the note carefully into her satchel, Alice headed towards the opening and gingerly stepped down into the cellar.

It was dank and cold and slowly moving behind her was Mrs Stanton. They could both hear footsteps above their heads, as if someone was pacing around the parlour. This was shortly followed by the sound of furniture being dragged across the parquet floor, etching reminders or sending a message. At the back of the cellar stood an old dilapidated bookcase, which looked as if it had seen better days. To one side of it was a stack of old papers, an old gramophone record player caked in thick dust and an old box sprouting mushrooms of some sort, exacerbating the growth of a variety of flora and fauna which had taken up residence and was thriving.

"I seem to remember, that when we first came here – that was back in our youth – Jasper and I had gone through a secret door which took us to some tunnels. I vaguely remember us following it and we somehow ended up underneath Leverstone Manor. We found all kinds of things down there, you just wouldn't believe it."

Trying to move things away, Mrs Stanton, who had appeared to be quite fragile, was now ripping away and casting aside everything near to the old bookcase. It also seemed that something was happening above them now too, and then they heard the thud of the parlour door being closed and the sound of a key being turned in a lock.

"I wonder what's going on up there? I hope that Barney and Jasper are okay. It all seems a bit cloak and dagger if you ask me. But what do I know? It's as if it's all quite normal, Mrs Stanton, to you."

Mrs Stanton turned to Alice and smiled, "Well, I suppose it is quite normal for us really, considering. Alice, you seem surprised by it all – Oh yes, we get regular visits from the Government – it's been going on for years – especially more so since Barney came back with Jasper from London. I think one of those up there is the old Major Buttertone-Smithe. I think that's his name."

Alice seemed mesmerized by Mrs Stanton.

Then from the far corner she spotted a chink of light filtering through the splinters of the bookcase. As they moved the bookcase aside Alice felt a sudden compulsion to retrieve the ball from her satchel. As she did it got jostled in the excitement of breaking through and rolled out of Alice's hands and forward and out into the opening before them. The piece of paper unfolded in the palm of Alice's hand it read   'FIND ME – IN LOVE AND LIGHT. B x'

# Chapter Eighteen
# Looking

Mrs Stanton and Alice squeezed themselves through the gap, their clothes ragged across the walls, which were rough and cold. The tunnel was dark and the walls wet with water from an unknown source.

Just before they both had stepped through into the darkness, Mrs Stanton had grabbed matches and an old lamp; the two scrabbled in the flints of light streaming from the cellar. After several attempts the lamp was lit and their way ahead was illuminated. Holding the lamp aloft Alice and Mrs Stanton scanned around them, there seemed to have been signs of life, if not now at least some time quite recently. The two decided to slowly make their way down the tunnel, stopping for breaks along the way. Mrs

Stanton had stashed water and provisions in an old shopping bag. Partway down the tunnel and beyond the opening in Jasper's cellar, a distant dot appeared on the passing horizon. Alice suddenly stopped; she was rummaging in her satchel tossing out the contents as she searched.

"Alice, is everything okay? You've been awfully quiet. Is something the matter? Do you know what we're meant to be looking for down here? What was the urgency and why is Barney with those people?"

Mrs Stanton had now started trying to help Alice pick up everything that had been strewn across the floor. A rat thought it may have been in for a steal as it scuttled across her foot. Mrs Stanton shrieked and kicked the rat, sending it flying across the tunnel passageway.

Alice quickly covered Mrs Stanton's mouth with her hand. "What are you doing? Do you want us to get caught or something? And as for being quiet, well, we need to be, don't we?"

Alice paused — her eye was being drawn to writing streaked across the wall. Written as if it had been scratched into the stone, the words read:

'From darkness comes light, from light comes life. You have the answer within the palm of your hand'.

Alice scribbled the words down.

"Mrs Stanton, what do you think it means? Do you think it's a sign or a clue? Oh, how I wish Barney was here now."

Alice turned sharply thinking she had heard Barney's voice – there was no Barney. It must have been her overwhelming expectation conjuring illusions.

Mrs Stanton, still unsure what was going on, looked confused and said, "Shall we carry on? Maybe we'll find our way out soon and Jasper's bound to wonder where I am as it must be near to tea time. I cannot be late; it always has to be on time."

Moving further down the tunnel it had started to appear to be getting lighter, the atmosphere was lifting and the feeling of suffocation was passing. Looking ahead of them they saw a few people darting about, they weren't dressed like they were though. Travelling down towards the changing scene, they felt apprehensive, fearful and unsure.

Stopping abruptly Alice said, "Mrs Stanton, who do you think they are? What if it's a trap of some kind? What will we do if we can never escape and get back to Barney and Jasper?"

Alice, now ravaged by her own fear, which prodded and poked at her heart, paused momentarily. In the stillness she closed her eyes and visualised the end game. She could see Barney, Ms Pemberton, Jasper, Mrs Stanton and her family and friends all very clearly. Everyone was smiling and life was how it should be. Oakley Place seemed a happier place to be and no signs of darkness anywhere. The emotion and joy of the vision in her mind's eye sent her crashing to the floor, her hands joined in soulful prayer.

Mrs Stanton just stared, "What are you doing, Alice? I think we'll need more than some wishful thinking and Divine intervention."

Just as Mrs Stanton had allowed the last word to drip from her lips, they had appeared to be even closer to the group of people ahead of them. It was as if they had been pulled along the tunnel by an invisible unseen force. A rather exuberant lady, a few children and two elderly looking gentlemen met them. They were dressed in 1940s attire.

The lady said, "Don't suppose you know if we're okay to go back now, do you? This air raid malarkey ain't no fun – these two old blokes also want to know if they can go back too."

Their dress was even older.

Alice and Mrs Stanton stared at each other in strange disbelief. The two of them made their excuses and, moving to one side, they bent towards each other and whispered, "What is happening? Why are they all acting as if they've been misplaced in time and why are they all in this tunnel?"

Alice stopped and looked, trying to figure out what they were going to say and trying to pull an answer from the air. Alice opened her satchel as if she was about to pull out a magician's wand to magic everything back into place.

The bunch of strangers gasped and looked baffled.

"What are you two doing? Are you trying to find your way out? Good luck to you both."

The lady was now moving towards them, "Sorry if we've spooked you both, this seems to happen every time. All's we want is to get home, that's all. The kids need to see their dad and as for those two old men, well – I'm not sure where they've come from, I can't seem to make a word out. Do you think you can get us out of here?"

The lady looked hopeful and smiled.

Alice now flicking through her book, hoping that she could find an answer within the pages of her book. Every page seemed to hold a grain of hope.

"Sorry, I have no answers yet, but let's see what we can do, shall we?"

She reached out towards the lady to offer her some reassurance. Mrs Stanton was playing pat-a-cake with the two young children and they seemed to be lost in childhood games.

The two elderly men shuffled forward and started to speak. Their language was interesting; Alice could not understand what they were trying to say. They pointed towards a diagram that had slipped from the pages of Alice's notebook. Alice was now trying desperately to try and decipher what they were trying to say to her. She watched them as they traced their fingers around the diagram; one had found a stick and was writing something in the dirt. Alice looked and realised the words were those she had seen in the book Barney had been showing her. If only Barney were here right now, he would be sure to have the answers. One of the men snatched the diagram and made a run for it towards what looked like an opening. He didn't seem to get very far and retreated back to where we had gathered. The second man seemed agitated and was waving his hands and ranting in their strange dialect.

"Mrs Stanton, what do you think we should do?"

Alice had her head back in the notebook. She was trying to figure out the words etched in the dirt. Remembering what Barney had said about it looking either Latin or that it may have been Sanskrit she tried to piece together each letter. What she saw in the dirt looked mystical and enchanting, words danced into place spelling out the following in the dirt before her: '**बृघ्त थे लिघ्त इन योउर् हेअर्त् शिनेस लिके थे बृघ्तेस्त सुन, दर्क्नेस्स हिदेस अन्द् अन्द् चान नो लोङ्गेर लिवे इन थे हेअर्त् ओफ़् लोवे'.**

The two elderly men, transfixed and intoxicated, danced in joy. The others came over, "Do you know what it says, Alice? Do you know what it means?" They all clambered around, the children gleefully dancing and erasing the words from the dirt as they tripped. The children had trampled most of the words away.

Alice stood to her feet; a moment of shaking realisation shook her to the core. Reaching back into her satchel, she tried to locate her mobile phone. "Mrs Stanton, I don't know why I didn't think about this before. I'm going to take a photo with my phone, and then I'm going to check it out on the Internet and see if I can find anything. We should be able to get a connection down here. What do you think?"

Everyone seemed to freeze.

Now they were the ones looking spooked. Alice held the mobile phone up in the air searching for an elusive reception.

"Alice, what on earth are you doing, and what is that thing in your hand? Put it away, it looks dangerous – what's that funny noise?"

Looking somewhat amused, Alice taunted Mrs Stanton waving the phone close to her face, "What's wrong with you? Look, it's a mobile phone, that's all, not some weird Stone Age device. You do know what a mobile phone is, don't you? It does seem that Oakley Place is lost in some crazy Bermuda Triangle type scenario thing."

Mrs Stanton came a little closer and tried to touch the mobile phone, as if she had never seen or heard of one before.

"Go on, hold it if it makes you feel better. It's out of date now and I'm getting a more-up-to date version for my birthday as it's going to be a special one."

The others had now edged forward and wanted to see what it was. The lady slowly walked forward and put out her hand, turning her head as if she did not want to see.

In relief she said, "Look everyone, I'm still alive, I think I am going to be fine – come over here, Charlie and Emily."

The children now reluctantly joined their mother.

The two elderly men also ventured forward, curious and intrigued.

Well, it was now getting late; the light in the tunnel was starting to fade. Mrs Stanton was wringing her hands and pacing. The others appeared to be losing interest in the mobile phone after an hour or two.

"Alice, did you hear that noise? I think I can hear men's voices. Do you think it may be Jasper and Barney looking for us? Oh, I do hope so, I want to go home."

The light rapidly dispersing and melting back into the walls, the lamp flickered as if it was about to splutter out.

Alice tried to peer down the tunnel behind them. She sounded tired, "I think we may have to sleep here tonight, Mrs Stanton. If it is Barney and Jasper I'm sure we'll be found. I need to sleep and in the morning I'll try and search the Internet on my mobile to see if I can find some answers."

# Chapter Nineteen
# Time Travellers

Jasper, Mrs Stanton, Barney and Alice watched as the rats scuttled about their feet, gorging themselves on remnants of leftovers.

"Funny little creatures really, such a shame they get so much bad press still – even after all this time. I bet things were different before the plague arrived on our pleasant English shores."

Alice was intrigued by the rats running around the tunnel scurrying for all their worth.

"Jasper, what do you know about the plague? You seem very knowledgeable about that period of time."

Alice sat; keen to learn what Jasper could impart.

"I find history and all that stuff so fascinating, and I'm incredibly interested in anything about the plague. It's part of the reason why I begged my poor parents to move nearby really. You see, I'd been researching the plague, and Oakley Place came up time and time again. I thought it was a bit odd but I kept on looking, I just knew there had to be a link of some kind to this place."

Alice looked at Barney, Mrs Stanton and Jasper's faces – they were captivated as she carried on.

"I also read somewhere on the Internet something about there being three vicars in Oakley, as it was back then, who all died in quick succession when the plague first hit the village. It stated that the plague had arrived in 1349."

Alice rummaged around in her satchel and pulled out a typed page on which was written the following information:

*'1327 John de Abingdon became the first vicar of Oakley (as opposed to rector). 1349 William de Grauntpont died in office as vicar of Oakley, probably of the Black Death. The first estimate of Oakley's population was made by Lysons, in 1377. In 1522 Oakley's population of men eligible for military service (ages 16–60) was estimated at 140. The oldest existing house in the village dates from around this time. In 1570 coppicing enclosures drew complaints from Richard Leigh of Oakley (Lord of Oakley).*

*In 1586 Oakley had about 248 inhabitants in 56 households (22 landholders and 58 with small cottages within the Forest). These figures were drawn up by Hugh Cope of Oakley in his Court of the Exchequer return'.*

Barney, Jasper and Mrs Stanton looked astounded. Could this have possibly been confirmation? Jasper and Mrs Stanton gave each other a nervous glance as if they were concealing something.

Alice asked Jasper if he could help with any other information, as when she had arrived in Oakley Place one of the villagers had said that Jasper would be the best person to speak to as he had lived in Oakley Place the longest. Alice, now in her element and glowing with excitement, was even more eager to absorb everything that Jasper could tell her.

"Wow! Jasper, you really are a mine of information. Please tell me some more – please."

Jasper, though tired and starting to feel drained, gladly obliged.

"Did you know that some folks have said that Frederick de Soames was some kind of time traveller? Personally speaking, I think that's all a load of old baloney. Made-up stuff to add a bit of glamour to his dark character. Alice, what else did you want to know about the plague and Oakley Place?"

Alice paused, thinking deeply – there was still so much more that she needed to know.

"I just want to know everything, Jasper, simply everything."

Jasper smiled and carried on, "Right, Alice, if my memory serves me right, didn't the plague start off in India? Everyone seems to think it was Europe, but I'm pretty sure it was in India, around the 1340s. I know for certain that the chronicler Henry Knighton wrote it in some book of the day. I think I may have a copy of it back in the house. Anyway, I digress. Henry Knighton wrote that the Black Death or the plague's origins had started in India and had then spread to Asia, affecting mainly Jewish and Christian populations. Some folk back then turned to pagan ways of life and trusted the Wise Ones. It then seemed to travel and arrived in Europe at the Sicilian City of Messina in October 1347. It was rapidly spreading out throughout the continents before it reached our little island of England. Although many think Frederick de Soames brought it here in the 1340s."

Mrs Stanton had started to doze off but Barney and Alice were hooked on Jasper's every word. Alice and Barney eagerly asked Jasper to carry on. Shifting his frail body, determined to carry on with his version of the history of the plague and the Black Death, Jasper was on a roll now. Like a stone gathering moss, he just couldn't stop. It was as if he'd swallowed a whole collection of books and had chomped them all down in one sitting.

Jasper started again after gulping down a glug of water.

"Did you know that the plague interrupted most social and commercial life during the day for almost 250 years? Did you also know that even William Shakespeare had written it into one of his plays – Romeo and Juliet? Apparently it's said that the following lines are ones that Shakespeare's audiences in the day would have understood:

*'Friar John:*

*One of our order, to associate me,*

*Here in this city visiting the sick,*

*And finding him, the searchers of the town,*

*Suspecting that we both were in a house*

*Where the infectious pestilence did reign,*

*Seal'd up doors, and would not let fourth.*

***William Shakespeare, Romeo and Juliet, Vii'***

Alice and Barney sat in stunned silence.

How did Jasper know so much about the plague?

Questions started to float between them almost on telepathic waves.

Jasper started up again, relishing in his captive audience's gaze.

"In the *'Decameron'*, Giovanni Boccaccio had written that the effects of the plague or Black Death had majorly impacted on Florence; more than half of the population may have perished in the epidemic of 1348. Many folks thought that was where Frederick de Soames may have travelled from Italy. Boccaccio wrote that most of the victims had died within just three days after the appearance of swellings, or buboes, in the groin or armpit, which were the first signs of the plague. He also wrote that it had seemed to be passed on from person to person by simply conversing with someone afflicted with the vile plague, and that is why it was so virulent. Even just touching clothes could have been fatal. Medical quacks of the day were at a complete loss and could not find a cure. It was quite common for folks to carry nosegays of flowers or herbs to ward off the stench and foul odour of the plague.

Social practices of nursing those sick with the plague had many connotations. Men were not allowed to look after women folk, and it was taboo for women to look after men folk too. As a result of this situation there seemed to have been a breakdown with simple burial practices too. Burying the dead bodies soon became chaotic and the whole order of burials and caring broke down. The poor dead had no burial rites as there was practically no time. Burials were not planned or long-drawn-out occasions as they are today."

Jasper paused again; looking to make sure his rantings had not bored Alice and Barney to tears. Barney and Alice were now drinking and had found some food and were making themselves quite comfortable.

Barney looked at Jasper and said, "Carry on, Jasper. You seem full of beans about this plague malarkey. Please, do carry on. I'm intrigued to learn more."

Alice nudged Barney and smiled at Jasper in a knowing way.

Jasper was now feeling weary. He said, "Alice and Barney, I may have to continue our history lesson another time. I need to have a rest. You've both worn me out."

Alice said, "Come on now, Jasper, just tell us some more, please – I just can't get enough."

Jasper had just sat down and looked at Alice and Barney, "Okay, here you go but we should maybe think about waking Mrs Stanton and heading back upstairs. But I will carry on for a little longer if it keeps you both quiet? So, burials were not planned – the families would have usually followed on after the deceased loved one, but now burials were a free-for-all – usually attended by strangers, who were often themselves victims of the plague. Due to the large number of deaths, especially here in Oakley Place, the consecrated burial grounds were filling up quickly and the Wise Ones, or Twitchers as you Barney and Alice call them, ended up having to dig huge mass graves on unconsecrated ground. Barney, the graves are on the map of the burial site. Although I'm not sure you'll find it though. Some graves were even dug under the ground in this very tunnel, under houses, under lots of places in Oakley Place. You see, Barney and Alice, we were running out of space – as most of us were perishing."

# Chapter Twenty
# The Guardians of Time and Space

Jasper was now standing next to Mrs Stanton. Something had changed; the atmosphere in the tunnel seemed charged with an invisible energy.

Jasper said, "You see, Barney and Alice, we had to dig them, to take care of the plague victims. We were like the death beaters in London."

Barney's ears pricked up at this comment, "Jasper, can I stop you right there, please! What do you mean, 'we', and that you were running out of space to bury the plague victims' bodies? The way you say it, Jasper, you make it sound as if you and Mrs Stanton were actually around at that time. Boy, that's freaky, Jasper, don't you think? Old man, that's just too weird. If that were the case then well, you would both be, well, old! Alice, I think he's just pulling our leg and trying to wind us both up. Well, you are really, aren't you, Jasper and Mrs Stanton?"

Jasper was quiet. He looked at Mrs Stanton. The air pressure in the tunnel suddenly dropped. It was as if the ceiling was about to cave in on their heads. Barney and Alice panicked. It felt as if their breath was being sucked out. Jasper and Mrs Stanton stood motionless, just staring.

"Barney and Alice, I think Mrs Stanton and I need to explain a few things to you both. Please listen. We know that you'll probably think we've flipped or gone batty in our old age – but here goes. Mrs Stanton and I are the Wise Ones. Do you remember – we are those people that Ms Pemberton talked to you about? We are the elderly couple who made the talismans and created the Twitchers. Yes! It was us. You see, we cannot die or leave Oakley Place until Frederick de Soames is no more."

Jasper and Mrs Stanton's demeanour had changed again. As they stood there they no longer seemed old, but stood tall and strong and were more assertive.

"Barney, when I saw you at the back of the old Government building, something inside made me think that you were the one that had been written across time and space, the one who would stop time itself and reset the passage of time bringing us all hope and delivering us from the blackest of darkness and Frederick de Soames' curse. I just knew you were the one. I rang Mrs Stanton and told her all about you and said that I had been sure you would be the help we needed. There was no uncertainty in our minds and that's when we decided that we had to get you back here and off the streets. It seems that from your arrival here, Barney, that the portal of time was re-opened and you are indeed the one to bring things to an end."

Barney and Alice laughed their heads off as if it was some sick joke. Barney stopped laughing for a second or two and noticed that something unusual was happening. Alice prodded him sharply and was trying to get him to ask Jasper a question. She seemed to have lost her nerve.

Barney opened his mouth and words spilled out, "You've got to be joking, Jasper. You're having a laugh, right Jasper, old man? I mean you are, aren't you?"

Barney started to feel unsure about what was now unfolding, the nervousness in the pit of his stomach waging a war within.

Their gaze seemed to bury into his chest. Alice too had stopped laughing and was now staring uncomfortably at Jasper and Mrs Stanton. Looking around, Barney and Alice tried to think what they were going to do.

Barney whispered to Alice, "What if Jasper and Mrs Stanton are not lying? What if this has been a set-up? What if it's all actually true? What are we gonna do, Alice?"

Jasper and Mrs Stanton moved closer. At first, Barney and Alice reacted by trying to pull themselves away. It was as if they were being pulled yet again by some strange invisible force. Jasper and Mrs Stanton put their arms around Barney and Alice's shoulders.

Mrs Stanton and Jasper leaned in saying, "Barney, Alice, it's all going to be okay. You're both safe. It will all take time to sink in. Once you've both got your bearings, all will be well again. All you both need is just a little more time to let this all sink in. We understand how you both must now feel."

Barney and Alice felt the sensation of heat; it was at that very moment that they both truly understood everything.

# Chapter Twenty-One
# Transitions

Up above them in the village, a major shift in the equilibrium of the place had created change. What had happened at the precise moment in time when Jasper and Mrs Stanton had landed their surprise revelation had now created a ripple across time.

Ms Pemberton stood on the village green; she was looking around trying to find Barney. As the sun blistered down Ms Pemberton attempted to seek the solace of shade under the old oak tree. Someone at some time had carved the initials of their love on the bark of the tree. The initials were MP and BL, which had been carved within the centre of a love heart shape. Ms Pemberton wondered who had carved it, and if by some quirk of fate young love and the creator of the symbol of love were still together.

The carving had set her thinking about Barney.

Now that Martin Fothergill had disappeared it was difficult for her to move on with life. Ms Pemberton felt lost and alone; his departure had left a vacant space. Ms Pemberton's heart ached for love and Barney had been a constant friend in troubled times. She missed his smile, his crazy ramblings and wacky ideas. Slumping down, Ms Pemberton sat within the protruding roots at the base of the ancient oak tree. The heat of the sun was sweltering. Taking off her jacket and placing it untidily on the ground beside her, she basked in the coolness of the shade.

A car pulled up suddenly outside the house of Jasper and Mrs Stanton. The occupants of the vehicle were wearing suits and looked quite official. From a distance one of the men who had exited the vehicle stepped forward scanning the area, his behaviour suspicious and shifty.

Ms Pemberton peeked around the trunk of the tree. Watching carefully she wondered who they were, and what they were doing poking around in Oakley Place. Ms Pemberton also wanted to know why they were invading the home of two elderly people.

One of the two men was burly in stature and hammered forcefully on Jasper's front door. In the meantime the second individual was on his tiptoes trying to peek through the front window. Unfortunately his attempts to look in were halted by the netting across the window, which acted like a barrier and obscured his view. Clearly determined, he wheeled the dustbin over near to the window and proceeded to climb on top of the bin.

Ms Pemberton moved to get a better view. Thinking quickly she took pictures with her mobile phone, capturing the assailants in progress. In a few minutes Ms Pemberton had emailed the pictures to an old colleague from the Government team that she had been assigned to. Her thought was that it might shed some light on the identity of the individuals. Taking a quick glance back towards Jasper and Mrs Stanton's house she now saw both men trying to gain entry to the house. The two men were now looking around to see if anyone had noticed their antics.

Ms Pemberton quickly hid herself behind the oak tree. After a few minutes she heard the sound of glass being smashed. Looking up from her mobile phone, she was almost at the point of willing an email response from her friend in the Government department. Aside from that, Ms Pemberton was also now keen to make sure that Jasper and Mrs Stanton were in the house and that they were both all right.

Little did Ms Pemberton know she was above their heads, as Jasper, Mrs Stanton, Alice and Barney were now somewhere beneath her feet, travelling through the tunnels, which spun out like a web underneath the whole of Oakley Place. In the tunnel below her feet, Jasper, Mrs Stanton, Alice and Barney were now travelling further into the tunnel once more.

Changes were happening now on many levels and planes of existence, which radiated out in numerous directions. Looking up now towards what was Barney's bedroom window, Ms Pemberton could see two shadowy figures who looked as if they had been trying to draw across the curtain to conceal whatever it was that they were doing. Ms Pemberton wondered what they were up to, and she was also desperate to know what it was they were looking for.

The two men were in the house for some time before Ms Pemberton, concerned for the well-being of Jasper and Mrs Stanton, decided to fight her fear and bravely enter in through the slightly open front door. Her lightning-speed reaction may have been crucial in saving the lives of Jasper and Mrs Stanton. Just as fear had pulsated through her veins, it now dragged her forward and through the front door.

Ms Pemberton was now in the hallway. The doors of the living room and parlour had been left wide open. Above her she could hear the two men moving furniture around and dropping things to the floor, which thudded above a nervous Ms Pemberton's head. It was very clear that they were searching for something, but why were they in Barney's room in particular, of all places?

Suddenly a door banged shut upstairs and Ms Pemberton could hear movement at the top of the flight of stairs, as if one of the men may have been descending any minute. In her haste, and wrapped in the grip of fear once more, Ms Pemberton remembered where the cellar was. If she could just get there, she may have been able to hide until the two men upstairs had decided to leave. After glancing around the hallway Ms Pemberton noticed what had looked like an opening, the edge still sharp from when Jasper had, had to break through the boarding that had concealed it on the day when Frederick de Soames had paid a visit to Jasper's house. Squeezing through the hole, shaped almost like a door, Ms Pemberton then slowly walked down the flagstone steps into the depths of the cellar. Moments later she heard the two men rapidly descending the flight of stairs, and rampaging through all the rooms. Ms Pemberton breathed a heavy sigh of relief that her quick actions had aided her lucky escape.

Down in the depths of the cellar it was pitch black, the sound of scuttling and squeaks from the mice and rats added to her sense of unease. Ms Pemberton attempted to survey the area by reaching forward, feeling her way around the cluttered space. As she fumbled around the edges of the claustrophobic room she felt a sudden sharp breeze, which caught her unawares. As her hand reached out in front of her, she met with the sharp edges of what she thought may have been an old bookcase. Nearer the side of the old bookcase, Ms Pemberton felt the sudden rush of cooling breeze, which brushed against her skin gently. Now in front of her she sensed an opening. Driving back the resurgence of fear she knew she had to enter into this unknown space. Tentatively stepping slowly forward, Ms Pemberton hoped that she would make it out without being found. She also wondered if now in this unknown place she might find answers. Would she now see what had blinded her for so long?

# Chapter Twenty-Two
# The Cavalry

Alice tried to peer down the tunnel behind them. She sounded tired and a little lost, "I think we may have to sleep here tonight, Mrs Stanton. If it is Barney and Jasper I'm sure we'll be found. I need to sleep and in the morning I'll try to search the Internet on my mobile to see if I can find some answers."

The temperature dropped dramatically, our breath visible in wispy clouds. In the freezing cold, water slid down the walls.

The two children and their mother, who we had discovered was called Miriam. Stood looking on vacant and frozen in space, as if trapped in some strange time loop.

I wondered if it was Barney, and if it was, how close he was?

Further down the corridor Barney and Jasper were making headway, although Jasper was struggling to keep up. Barney had to slow down at least several times, in order for Jasper to keep up.

"Barney, are you sure we're heading in the right direction?"

Both men had been determined to find Alice and Mrs Stanton. What they hadn't realised was how long they had been trying to shake off Major Buttertone-Smithe and his able assistant – bizarrely it wasn't Ms Pemberton. The Major had not seen her for many months.

Fortunately, I had hidden my rucksack in the cupboard under the stairs. The hiding place was not obvious and it would have taken a genius to figure out its whereabouts. Anyway even in the hurry I managed to hide it without anyone noticing. I heard Jasper call out, and not wanting to appear rude, I'd ventured into the parlour. I heard Alice but thought she was chatting to Mrs Stanton. The Major and his assistant were making one of their routine visits. Jasper and I were asked a never-ending stream of questions; the level of invasiveness made me feel that my privacy was being eroded.

"How long have we been walking? I'm going to have to take a break, I'm exhausted. I think today has really caught up with me. Barney, look at this."

Jasper bent down to pick up a scrap of paper. Tottering forward with an unsteady gait, he found himself grappling and grabbing hold of the wall to ease himself to an upright position. The scrap of paper had a number printed along the edge.

Barney recognised that it looked like a fragment of one of the pages from Alice's notebook.

"Jasper, it looks like they may have been here. This fragment of paper is defo from Alice's notebook."

Barney put the scrap of paper in his jacket pocket.

"I wonder how long they've been gone. Do you think we'll find Alice and Mrs Stanton, Barney?"

Striding ahead, Barney, determined to find both of them, could not hear Jasper's mutterings and was eager to find Alice and Mrs Stanton as soon as possible. Jasper trailed behind and was now slowly making some progress — although desperate in his attempts to keep up with Barney.

"Barney, slow down, please, otherwise you're going to end up leaving me behind."

Jasper's voice bounced off the cold stone walls of the tunnel.

"I can't hear you, Jasper. What's up? Come on, catch up, haven't got all day, old man."

Barney waved at Jasper, who was slipping back into the distance again.

Alice and Mrs Stanton were woken by the sound of footsteps grazing the earth. Mrs Stanton was the first to sit bolt upright, followed by Alice.

"About time, I'm gonna go look to see if they're near."

Standing up and grabbing her satchel, Alice was off and heading towards the voices travelling up the tunnel. Starting to pick up speed, she shouted, "Come on, Mrs Stanton, I think they're really near."

Mrs Stanton stumbled to her feet, struggling to gain her balance.

"Mrs Stanton, come on! We've gotta get moving and find out if it is them and not some crazy illusion."

Meanwhile, Barney was racing towards them and Jasper was merrily tottering along at a snail's pace.

"Barney, how long do you think we've been down here, only I'm starting to feel a bit peckish?"

He looked at his watch. "See, I told you, lad, we should be heading back – it's almost tea time."

Barney muttered under his breath, "Jasper, what are you talking about? How can it be tea time? That's so ridiculous — when we set off it was only morning. We can't have lost that much time."

Alice and Mrs Stanton were storming forward – excited at the mere prospect of being reunited with Barney and Jasper. They were also keen to get back home. Barney and Jasper had caught up with each other again.

"Jasper, I think I can see them — Alice and Mrs 'S' – look, they don't seem to be that far away."

Jasper looked but his eyesight was failing and his advancing years had taken their toll.

"Is that you, Alice, is Mrs Stanton with you?"

The four were now almost within touching distance.

"Barney, can you hear me? We've found some others down here."

Barney was looking at the map. He had also taken out the book and had found the first symbol, which matched one etched on the tunnel wall.

"Alice, I've found a clue – I think there may be a few more down here. Let's see if we can find them."

Alice came over to see what Barney was doing.

"Do you need my help, Barney? Two heads are always better than one."

Alice and Mrs Stanton were now standing with them. Smiling at Barney in relief, Alice leaned in close to speak, "Barney, do you have your talisman?" She also spoke in a silent tone to Jasper and Mrs Stanton. Barney threw the second talisman to Alice, who quickly placed it around her neck. Jasper and Mrs Stanton had put their talismans on too.

"Alice, why do we need to put them on? What's with the urgency?"

Alice opened her satchel to retrieve her notebook – "I think I may be able to add to that."

She opened her notebook and guided Barney's eyes to the Sanskrit message. Before the two children had trampled the message out of the dirt, she had managed to scribble some of the symbols down.

"I'll just get my mobile too. I think I also grabbed a couple of pics of it." Scrolling through the selfies and random pictures on her mobile Alice finally found the message the two old men had written in the dirt. "Here it is – you see, this may be useful. What do you think, Barney?"

Barney and Jasper looked at the image, which was a bit blurry on the screen of the mobile phone.

"Do you know what it is supposed to mean, Alice?" Barney looked intrigued, "So how do you know what it says, Alice? How do you know how to read Sanskrit, Alice? I mean, it's a bit off the wall, if you don't mind me saying!"

Trying to reassure Barney that she knew exactly what she was talking about Alice said, "My folks took me to India, it's one of the downsides I suppose – my dear old mum is a practising Buddhist and it's kinda got ingrained – totes, forgot all about that stuff until now really – silly, but it all just came flooding back as if I were there yesterday."

Alice smiled at Barney, who was entranced.

"I'm all ears, Alice – we need to figure out what it's supposed to say – do you have any idea? There is something like it written in the book. Do you think it may be the other half of this page that has been torn out of the book?"

Alice took out her notebook again and flicked through the pages, "There, I've found it – well, I think it says something like, 'The bright light in your heart, shines bright. Darkness hides and can no longer live in the heart of love.'

I may be wrong – after all I'm no super language boffin – I've just picked bits up from here and there, that's all."

Barney took out his notebook and a pen and set to scribble down the translation. "What does it mean – did you see that flash of light ahead?" Jasper and Mrs Stanton were looking where Barney was pointing. A light flashed ahead of them again, this time it appeared to be closer. They all felt as if they were being drawn towards the light emission.

It felt like the pull of a strong magnet, which seemed to be drawing them towards the growing brightness and the centre of the light. Barney quickly grabbed the book and map. Alice had picked up all of her bits and pieces and was throwing them back into to her satchel.

"Jasper, Mrs Stanton, stay close by and follow me and Alice. We need to stay close together now. Have you noticed that it has started to feel a lot warmer down here and almost as if the light switch has been flicked on? I can see everything now – Oh, my goodness! There it is."

Barney rushed over to more writing, which was now visible on the wall. He had also spotted a door to one side and then there were even more tunnels all shooting off in different directions.

"Which way do you think we should head down, Alice? Are we anywhere near to the people you were talking to me about?"

Alice and Mrs Stanton paused, bending down. Alice picked up a little wooden doll. "They're not here anymore, but they were right here – look, here's the little girl's doll."

She held the doll out towards Barney.

"Are you sure? It may have been a trick of the light."

Turning to Mrs Stanton, Alice encouraged Mrs Stanton to speak.

"Barney, Alice is right. There were two children. I think they were called Charlie and Emily. Their mother was called Miriam and there were also two elderly foreign-looking men. They were definitely here – we played pat-a-cake, me and the children, and sang songs just like when we were kids, Jasper." Mrs Stanton, Jasper, Alice and Barney all looked around them to see if they could find any remnants of the people Alice and Mrs Stanton had met. Jasper and Mrs Stanton sat down against the wall – both weary and fighting sleep.

"Alice, I think it's just going to be the two of us for now – they're clearly struggling to keep up. Do you have any food, that we can leave behind with them until we can get back?"

Looking in her satchel and in Mrs Stanton's bag, she said, "Do you think that's a wise idea? What if they disappear too? That would be dreadful. I'd miss them both if they weren't around."

Alice dropped food and water near the sleeping pair.

" To be honest with you, Alice, it's really not one of my greatest ideas, I know, but we can't waste any more time – going by what the Major told us, he thinks that Frederick de Soames and his entourage may be back again. We have to try to find the answers before then."

Standing shoulder to shoulder with Barney, Alice tried to catch Barney's eye – "Did you say anything about the Curtain Twitchers?"

Tearing a page from his notebook Barney scribbled a note to Jasper and Mrs Stanton. The words read:

*' Wait here. Do not wander off. Alice is with me and we're going to try to find the answers. We'll meet you back here before it gets dark. Stick to the tunnel and head back to the cellar if we're not back by then. We've left you a drink and some food for you both to share – Love to you both Barney and Alice xx.'*

Barney pushed the note into the top pocket of Jasper's jacket pocket. Travelling further down, they both felt the pull of the light. The talismans burnt red hot around their necks. In a darkened recess a dark figure stepped out towards the two, who had now stopped in their tracks.

"Who are you? We mean no harm."

Stepping out towards the brightness the figure put up a hand to shield its eyes from the bright light.

"Is that you, Martin Fothergill?"

A jumble of words came from his mouth. He was just as he had been that day back at Banthom's Biological Laboratory when he had been brought into the interview room. His deterioration now quite measurable, falling forward into them Martin Fothergill gasped for air – he was holding a folded piece of paper. He smelled disgusting, the stench of chemicals and rotting flesh mingled into the warm air.

"I don't understand how can you be down here, Martin. You were safely secured back at the lab – so how did you get down here? It makes absolutely no sense whatsoever. We must be miles away."

Alice tried to grab the paper, but was nervous in case something happened. She also did not want to touch Martin Fothergill in case she caught anything.

"Barney, what do you think we should do? How did he get here? What lab?"

Barney was now trying to move Martin Fothergill away from the light.

"Tell me again slowly, how did you end up here?"

Martin Fothergill pointed towards another tunnel leading off. As I looked down the tunnel I saw others – stepping back I did not want to appear scared even though I was freaking out inside.

"Alice, stay perfectly still – we need to either move forward or over to the dark recess near to Martin Fothergill – I'll explain in a few minutes – we don't have time to mess about, you see…"

Barney had been distracted. "I think we should be okay as long as we keep our talismans around our necks."

Alice felt around her neck; the talisman was missing.

"Barney, it's gone – oh no! What's gonna happen – it's got to be around here somewhere."

Grovelling around on the floor Alice tried to find the talisman.

"Barney, are you just gonna stand there or what? Come on, please help me find it – there's no way I'm gonna end up like that poor soul."

Alice gestured towards Martin Fothergill. "Come on, help me. What's that groaning noise, Barney?"

Frantically looking for the talisman, the two searched.

I sensed another presence close by, other than Martin Fothergill. I whispered to Alice, "I think we may be in trouble. There are others like Martin Fothergill, there down that tunnel. They seem to have escaped the lab."

Fear was etched across Alice's face. Trembling, she held onto Barney's arm, "What are we going to do? How have they managed to escape? I thought you said the lab was miles away – I think I may just cry – I'm so scared, I don't want to die."

Barney threw his arm around her shoulder.

"Alice, don't worry, I'll get us out of here somehow."

"Barney, what happens if we don't make it out? How are we gonna stop Frederick de Soames? What we gonna do, Barney?"

Alice was shaking.

Tears had started to stream down her face.

"Alice, I promise it's going to be okay. We need to keep our heads and focus. Right, just stay close."

As they started to move forward Barney kicked something metal, which he thought was an old coin as it spun up into the air and ricocheted, hitting off the wall. Alice reached up to catch it before it hit the ground. She caught it spinning in mid-air as she grasped its cold slippery surface. There appeared to be something written on the other side. Alice dashed into the light holding the item tight in her hand. Closer to the source of light, Alice examined the item and read the words written on the reverse, which was very clear to her as being written in old Latin. Barney was just about to step forward, when he noticed Alice. Before he had a chance to stop her reading the words, which were written on the metal disc, Alice was in full flow, speaking the words out loud. Each word: clear and precise. And the words were just as they were written:

*'Umbrae protegat, quos hide, ex lumine, sanctity affert, et lux a tenebris, Ipsae cadent, omnes qui, sub tutela, salvus erit'.*

In her excitement at remembering her Latin lessons, and feeling buoyed up by the whole experience. Alice read the words out even louder this time with more gusto and an air of authority as if she had been casting a spell:

*'UMBRAE PROTEGAT, QUOS HIDE, EX LUMINE, SANCTITY AFFERT, ET LUX A TENEBRIS, IPSAE CADENT, OMNES QUI, SUB TUTELA, SALVUS ERIT.'*

It now appeared to be getting brighter by the second and the figures cowered in the darkness, the light forcing them back into the receding shadows of the tunnel.

"Alice, what have you done? We now have to go back quickly – and I hope it's not too late – hopefully Jasper and Mrs Stanton will still be where we left them. We will have to hurry; by reading the talisman you have now set the wheels in motion for a shift in time and a massive change to all our lives for good or bad. Alice, by doing what you have done, things have been set in motion too soon – I am fearful of what the consequences may be."

Alice looked like a naughty child who had been disciplined severely by an overbearing parent.

"Barney, what have I done? Can we stop it? What do I need to do?"

I walked away back down the tunnel.

"Alice, are you coming before none of us make it out of here? I'm not about to sign my own death warrant. You may have slowed Frederick de Soames' return but could have unwittingly speeded up the demise of the Curtain Twitchers."

Alice looked around.

There was now little darkness and the dark figures had retreated into the tunnel's depths.

"Barney, wait for me, please – wait!"

Running now to try and keep up with Barney, Alice was desperate not to be left behind. Pacing ahead, Barney was miles ahead of Alice by now. He was still angered by her ill thought-out actions.

Alice shouted after Barney, "Stop! – Wait! – I know I made a huge mistake — I'm sorry! Please, Barney, give me another chance – please! We can do this together – you know we can."

*I could hear Alice, however, I was not prepared to risk losing Jasper and Mrs Stanton for the sake of her stupid mistake. It's true I could have warned her, I suppose she was not to know, so for that I should accept at least some of the blame, I suppose – right?*

"Wait! Barney, I'm scared. I think something may be following me, I'm too scared to look in case it's one of those things!"

Barney looked behind her. She was definitely being tracked by something, only maybe not by who or what she had feared.

Barney shouted, "There's a woman dressed in 40s attire following you, she just appeared out of the light. I think she's trying to speak to you?"

Now standing right behind Alice, who had frozen to the spot, the woman placed her hand on Alice's shoulder and said, "You told me you'd be back – where are you going? I've lost the others – not sure where the two children have vanished to – it's all your fault, Alice."

The woman's voice was ethereal and intermittent; as if she was been fragmented by the light, or maybe she had been a projection whose reception was suffering some kind of energetic interference. Looking puzzled, Barney stared in disbelief, as from the light appeared two children, who were closely followed by two extremely old and oddly dressed men.

"Alice, who are these people? Where have they come from?"

The two looked at each other unsure of what was unfolding before their eyes. Charlie, the young boy, rushed to Alice – looking around for Mrs Stanton.

"Hello – Where did you come from? Where is your little sister?"

He pulled hard on her hand, as if he was trying to tell her something.

"Oh, I see, you're looking for Mrs Stanton."

Watching on stood the little boy's mother and Barney.

"Alice, how do you know what he's saying? I cannot even hear a sound or see his little mouth moving. How do you know what he is saying? It's kinda weird and a bit spooky, if you ask me."

' *This was rich coming from Barney as he had witnessed much weirder events over the last month,' thought* Alice smiling.

A young girl had now also joined the young boy – the two children were trying to take Alice towards the light at the other end of the tunnel.

"No, I can't go that way. I've got to go that way with my friend, Barney – we're going to go and find Mrs Stanton and Jasper, our other friends. No, no, you can't come with me. Children, I have to go, we're running out of time. Best stay here with your mother. I promise I'll be back and I'll bring Mrs Stanton back to play games with you both. Won't that be fun?"

Barney was growing impatient and eager to really get on and find Jasper and Mrs Stanton. The light had appeared to also be changing and the luminance of the light was fading, rapidly. This made Barney worry that they might be a lot closer to fate, and that the endgame would not be what he wanted it to be.

"Alice, I have no idea how you're doing that but it's some neat party trick, for sure. Do you think you can leave them now, only we really do need to get to Jasper and Mrs Stanton as soon as we can? Let's go!"

Alice moved away from the children. The two clung to her like limpets even though their mother was standing close by. Extricating herself, Alice made a sudden dash to catch Barney. Barney and Alice made every effort to make their way up the tunnel and find Jasper and Mrs Stanton.

# Chapter Twenty-Three
# A World of Difference

Something hit them and not in the physical sense; it was more like the sudden realisation that things were changing but all too quickly. It was as if time was altering and shifting. They were both changing in looks too, and in their own thoughts and ways of thinking. Surrounded by a rapidly changing vista, Barney and Alice panicked. Rushing back down the tunnel the two saw visions of their lives as if time itself was unravelling.

"Alice, I think we may be too late."

Arriving at the precise spot where they had left Jasper and Mrs Stanton, there was now an empty void. Mrs Stanton and Jasper had vanished; the only reminders of them having been there were an empty bottle of water and the remnants of empty food wrappings.

"Oh no! What are we going to do? Where do you think they've gone? I wonder if they have set off back to the cellar as I told them to."

Barney looked hopeful that the elderly couple, who over time had given him so much love, support and kindness, in a way that had changed so much of his life for the better by taking him in and out of the darkness of life on the street.

Maybe the old couple had been smart and left a clue, or would that have been too easy a wish to make? Remembering and searching deep within he felt the pelt of sadness, restless in the pit of his stomach. He'd promised to be back, and against all of his best and most honourable intentions he had let them both down.

Feeling even more retched and deflated he glared at Alice, "If we hadn't messed about and you hadn't wanted to play stupid mind games with those two children and you had listened and done exactly as I had said, we would have got back in time. Alice, this is all your fault, everything — you're so selfish and so—"

Barney stopped.

He was furious with Alice, but he noticed tears flowing down her already tear-stained face.

"B-B-Barney, I know, I'm sorry – please don't get mad with me – I just wanted to help. You seem to have all of the answers. I promise from now on I'll do everything you say and I promise I will listen. Please, will you give me one last chance – please, Barney? I can't bear it if you say no!"

Barney threw his hands in the air, trying to hold his anger in as if trying to contain a wild beast.

"Alice, to be quite honest, this is your mess-up – if we had not taken so long and had just headed back, and if you had not read the words out loud from the back of the talisman. Do you get my drift, Alice? Do you understand why I am feeling so angry with you?"

Alice felt Barney's anger wrapping around her like a slippery snake, tightening around her trying to force out her last breath from her broken and fragile state of being.

"Barney, I said I'm sorry – I don't know what else I'm supposed to say? How can I put things right? How can I say the right words to make everything right, Barney? What do you want me to do?"

Darkness was now invading the tunnel spaces, merging the darkened recesses. Alice was down on her knees, broken and gasping for air.

"What's wrong with you now, Alice, cat got your tongue or something?"

Alice was silent.

She sat in the pitch-blackness of the tunnel, lost and alone. Barney's words pierced her skin, leaving scars and wounds. In deep thought, Alice remembered Barney how he was before – his joyfulness and happy-go-lucky ways.

What had happened to make him so heartless, so unforgiving?

"Well, Alice, what are you doing?"

Ahead of her stood Barney holding a flickering lantern aloft.

"We cannot stay here – it's time to go back to see if Jasper and Mrs Stanton made it back safely. Who knows, Alice, we may even get to enjoy one of Mrs Stanton's legendary cream teas."

Barney now appeared to have calmed down and was more like his old familiar self – he was even trying to make light of their situation, cracking witty jokes and battering banter about the place.

"Are you coming, Alice? Sorry, I'm not sure what just happened but we haven't got time to rest on our laurels now, have we?"

He smiled and gave her a friendly reassuring wink.

Alice slowly stood up, she felt bruised and battered by the whole ordeal. Maybe this had been some kind of payback or Divine retribution for what she had done.

"Barney, I'm coming – Yes! Yes! Let's go and find Jasper and Mrs Stanton, shall we? It will be good to get back to Oakley Place at last."

The two of them walked together down the tunnel towards the cellar opening.

## Chapter Twenty-Four
## Finding the Truth

Back in Oakley Place, time had shifted. Nothing was as it had been, past or present. The curtains around hung motionless. Doors were closed, leaving a chilling eerie quietness, which seemed to envelop the whole village. Even the birds had ceased to sing their joyous peels of happiness, which always brought joy to the soul and eased a troubled mind.

Barney and Alice were now both back at the opening and squeezing themselves through the narrow gap. As they entered the cellar they disturbed a family of mice sending them scuttling across papers strewn across the surfaces thick with dust. Moving gingerly they tried not to knock teetering boxes and the piles of detritus around the place. Above them they could hear footsteps walking across the floor of what would have been the parlour, which was now placed above their heads.

Reassured, they both moved towards the steps of the cellar, hopeful and expectant to see Jasper and Mrs Stanton again. They both envisaged a joyful reunion and great times ahead.

Happy to be back and hopeful that they may have put the worst behind them, both of them were now optimistic that they may have also got back in time, before Frederick de Soames had made his return.

Now at the top step they could hear the familiar chatter of Jasper and Mrs Stanton. Drifting through the cellar door they slowly walked, trying not to break the flow of the voices or disturb their patter. Almost at the door, Alice dropped the talisman, causing it to spin across the parquet floor before clattering to a halt at the foot of the grandfather clock, which was primed and ready to chime as it had always done on the hour. You could set your watch by it.

Alice tried to shuffle across the floor to retrieve the talisman without making an enormous amount of noise. Barney put his finger to his lips as if to shush her, raising his hand in an attempt to get her to stop.

Alice crabbed back to Barney's side and whispered, "Sorry, Barney, I didn't mean to drop the talisman. Why aren't we just going in? This is weird even for you, Barney. You would normally be in there by now all guns blazing and all that jazz."

Barney seemed to hesitate; if they went in they may be walking into yet another drama. He had also caught the tail end of Jasper and Mrs Stanton's conversation. But more than that he had heard another voice. It was painfully familiar and he did not want to see who it belonged to. Alice was impatient and in her eagerness barged her way into the parlour, bursting through the door like an exploding Christmas cracker.

Only what was the surprise?

Standing in the parlour, Alice scanned the room, gracefully smiled at the woman and man sitting on the old sofa and sidled up to Jasper and Mrs Stanton who were sitting in their chairs.

"So, what's happening, Jasper? Who are the visitors? Come on, Barney – you coming in or what?"

Barney hovered near to the door reluctant to go in, knowing that he may be coming face-to-face with his parents.

"Alice, did you say that Barney was outside the door? Barney, are you there? We've got some people to see you here – I think you'll be in for a pleasant surprise. Come, what are you messing about at out there? Do I have to come and drag you in?"

Barney ran off up the stairs, and dived into his bedroom bolting the door behind him and dragging everything to the back of the door like a barrier. He sat down hard on his bed, and looked down at his feet. He had hoped that this day would never come and had been pushing and batting it from side to side, creating an internal tennis match in his mind. Only, set points may have just happened.

Alice had run out into the hallway and Barney could hear her calling, "Barney, where have you gone? I've met your folks – they're pretty cool if you don't mind me saying so. They asked me to come and have a break with you and them once you're back home and settled. Come on, Barney – what's all the fuss about? You must be mad – what you waiting for? I wish my folks were half as nice and all that."

' *It would have been easy to just go down and meet them, sit and have tea and reminisce about the good old days. But it would not really be like that. It may start out like that, be all lovey-dovey and sweet and then bang! I'd probably be landed a slap or two, she that is my mum would start screaming, and before you knew it dad would be downing a bottle of port and we'd be back to square one. That was one of the many reasons I had decided back then when I was about 14 years old to run away. I knew it would have been a darn sight safer than living with them, and besides, I had practically looked after myself since I was ten years old.'*

Barney stared out of the window trying to pluck answers from thin air. If he went downstairs he'd be confronted by Jasper, Mrs Stanton, Alice making goofy faces and his parents putting on the desperate doting parent act. He heard someone stomping up the stairs. They rattled at the door forcefully.

"Barney, are you in there? Are you coming out or do I have to come in and drag you down? Your poor parents have been here for hours and look quite tired; they've had a bit of a journey trying to get here. It seems that doctor Saunders found out where they lived and made contact. Barney, don't be hiding in there – come out, I'm sure things will get sorted. They seem lovely people, not at all how I thought they'd be – Barney, are you in there? Answer me, please."

Jasper had also now been joined by Alice. Between them both they pushed the door partially open. Barney jumped to his feet, startled by their entrance into his room. Before either of them had a chance to open their mouths

Barney jumped in with both feet. Shaking he said, "If you seriously think I'm coming downstairs with either of you, you can forget it! Nothing or no one could ever make me go back to that life. So if you think for one measly minute that I'm coming down to make up with those people who claim to be my so-called loving parents – you are so wrong!"

Barney seemed agitated, behaving like a little boy. Neither Jasper nor Alice, had seen him in such a terrible state as this before.

"Okay – what's wrong, Barney? Why won't you see your mum and dad? I just don't get it at all."

Alice looked mystified by Barney's reluctance to see his parents. She wondered what the fuss was really about, as did Jasper. Sitting Barney down back on the bed, they waited a few moments for him to calm down and explain.

"Jasper and Alice, okay, I'm ready now to tell you why I'm not going downstairs while they're here. You see, they may seem lovely and quite normal to you both but it's all an act. You do know that, don't you?"

Jasper and Alice looked concerned.

"Barney, what are you actually trying to say? Is there anything else you want to tell us?"

Barney squirmed in his sitting position; he was restless and emotional. "Promise me though, Jasper, you'll not make me go down to see them – I would rather die than do that. You see, those two people made my life a living nightmare from about the age of ten. Before that they were fab parents – the best in fact any one could have ever had. Then after my sister died in odd circumstances…"

He stopped and tried to swallow back the pain, before carrying on.

"I did not even know her really. She lived with my gran somewhere down on the coast; none of my family seemed to know where though. I get the feeling from bits I heard, especially when they were having heated arguments sometimes, that she was a love child from one of dad's flings. Anyway, something happened. To try and mask the pain of her loss, they filled their lives with work – forgot about me as if I were an afterthought. I ended up looking after myself pretty much most of the time. There would be days when they just didn't come back, leaving me to fend for myself. I would have to hunt around for food in bins just to get by. When they did come home, they'd make such a fuss of me and say how sorry they were. They would fill me up with lies and tall stories, overload me with expensive gifts and presents to try and make it up to me and to put their own minds at rest – there was no love! As

I got older the pressure seemed to start taking its toll on the pair of them and that's when they started to take their frustration and anger out on me."

Jasper sat stunned, a solitary tear glistened on his wrinkled skin. Alice's face was drenched in tears.

"Oh, Barney, I never realised. You never seemed to make me think that had happened to you. Why did you not say anything?"

Jasper and Alice looked at one another; they were clearly shaken.

"Say something – please, Jasper, Alice – What are we going to do? Please do not make me go down. If you do I'll swear that I'll make a run for it and I'd never come back – that's how much I hate them both. I thought that one day I'd feel differently about them, that I could go back home and carry on with life and things and for it to be just like it was when I was a young kid. Alice, that's why I was a bit edgy when I saw those kids with you the other day – it suddenly brought back memories of me with my parents when things were good, well, all those memories all came flooding back."

Jasper and Alice were chatting to each other now, out of earshot of Barney; they were discussing what they could do.

Mrs Stanton was now standing at the foot of the stairs. She called up to Jasper, "Jasper love, is Barney coming down? Only his parents are eager to get him back home and Barney's dad was just saying that if they don't leave soon they're going to get stuck in rush hour traffic. Just wanted to make sure everything is okay? Shall I say that he'll be down in a few minutes, Jasper? Will you get Barney's things together as well, Jasper, please? Bring them down, will you, when he comes down. Best not keep them too long, eh?"

Jasper and Alice turned to Barney – "Barney, it seems like they're pretty keen you take you with them. I'm not sure one hundred per cent what we should do. I only know that I cannot have you go back to live on those rat-infested streets in London again. I remember how you were, Barney, when you first arrived back with me here. You were in a dreadful way for months – wouldn't even come out of your room – spent most of your nights either pacing the floor, and when you weren't wearing the carpets out, you'd be screaming in your sleep and saying such awful things in your sleep – it made me cry! Don't worry, Barney, leave it to me – I'll sort this out and me and Alice will get rid of the two of them."

Alice nodded and smiled at Barney.

"So, Jasper, what exactly are we going to do?"

Jasper was now trying to offer reassurance to Barney.

Jasper could hear Mrs Stanton making her way up the stairs slowly, the steps creaked and she seemed to miss a step.

"Mrs Stanton, just go back into the parlour. We'll be down soon. Alice and I are just trying to sort some boxes that have fallen over in Barney's room, we're busily picking up some of his things. He's so messy, that kid. That noise we heard earlier must have been these boxes falling over. Best tell Barney's parents they might have had a wasted journey – the lad's not here. I've looked and he's definitely nowhere to be seen. He's perhaps nipped out to catch up with Harold and Reginald. You know how those boys like to mess about."

Jasper, Alice and Barney heard Mrs Stanton muttering to herself under her breath. And then she stumbled back into the parlour, banging the door hard behind her. It was at that point they heard raised voices coming from the parlour. Jasper looked worried and headed towards the door, shouting down to Mrs Stanton hoping that she may hear him.

She came back out and shouted back up to Jasper, "Are you definitely sure Barney isn't up there with you? Mr and Mrs Lumsden are adamant that they are taking Barney back with them and they're refusing to go anywhere without him. I thought Alice had said that he was just out near the door of the parlour before she came in?"

Barney was now scrabbling about trying to gather all his things together. Jasper and Alice were trying to get him to stop.

"Barney, just slow down – don't panic we will get you out – won't we, Jasper?"

Alice looked hopeful at Jasper. She leaned in and whispered, "How are we going to do it?"

Jasper quietly spoke to Alice, "We need to create some kind of diversion. I should go downstairs and calm things down – as soon as you hear me close the parlour door, you come down with Barney. Barney needs to head back down the cellar and wait for me in the tunnel until the coast is clear, while you open the front door and act as if someone has asked for the Lumsdens to move their car. Do you get that, Alice and Barney? It's the only way I can see us killing two birds with one stone."

They heard footsteps again heading upstairs – Jasper darted quickly like a whippet under starter's orders – he left the room and met Mrs Stanton who was almost at the top step, "Hello, my love, I'm just coming down – let's go back down to the Lumsdens as we don't want to them to think we're rude, do we?"

Mrs Stanton was suspicious; she could see someone moving about in Barney's room.

"So, who's that then, Jasper, in Barney's room? Who is it Jasper?"

Jasper tried to divert Mrs Stanton's gaze, he didn't want her to catch sight of Barney and blow everything, nor did he want to try to explain everything while Barney's parents were present.

Jasper successfully diverted Mrs Stanton, and had started to talk to her about what they were going to do to celebrate their special anniversary, which was fast approaching.

Jasper and Mrs Stanton went into the parlour. Jasper turned and gave a signal to Alice who was peeking out of Barney's bedroom door. Alice and Barney heard the firm snap of the door closing.

"Come on, Barney, this is your only chance if you're sure you don't want to go back with your parents."

Barney picked up his things and they slowly crept downstairs, trying to avoid the creaky steps, and made their way carefully back to the cellar, just as Jasper had instructed. Barney tripped down the cellar steps, and put his hands out in front of him to stop himself falling forward and headlong into the stack of delicately balanced boxes. Alice made a quick dash to the kitchen and was raiding the larder, stuffing crisps, cheese, bread, chocolate and anything she thought would be edible into a plastic bag. She also grabbed a few bottles of water and rushed down into the cellar to drop these with Barney.

After leaving Barney she made a fast track to the front door. She knew time was ticking for Jasper and she would play her part as he had asked by pretending to answer the front door. She spoke very loudly as if she was having a heated argument with someone, even though no one was actually there. She then rushed into the parlour and said that the Lumsdens would need to come as they were blocking someone's drive. Alice also kept a watchful eye on the cellar, and had covered the opening across with an old blanket, just in case Barney had not got into the tunnel yet. The Lumsdens didn't seem convinced with Alice's rouse but they also did not want to create a scene with the elderly couple, as the little charade may have backfired on them.

# Chapter Twenty-Five
# Reunited Souls

Ms Pemberton stood in the pitch-blackness of the open space before her. Stumbling along she felt the tunnel wall wet and cold upon her hand. The cool breeze now met a rush of hot air as if the door to an invisible furnace had been opened. Drifting slowly along, Ms Pemberton smelt the familiar smells of home and safety, reminding her of her childhood. Ahead, the darkness was lifting and her eyes were now able to define the edges of the place.

Further ahead, Barney, Mrs Stanton, Jasper and Alice had found another door.

In the distance some way back from where they now stood in the tunnel, Ms Pemberton was now surveying her surroundings, guided forward by a growing light which illuminated her footsteps.

Travelling now towards the light and traversing the dark, Ms Pemberton suddenly felt reassured and as if she was not alone. The light now wrapped around her like a comfort blanket. Pausing, she watched as the light now danced in front of her as if prompting her to follow it. At that moment she felt overwhelmed with love, her heart open and ready to accept her fate. In the distance she thought she had noticed a light ahead.

Back outside the locked door Jasper, Barney, Mrs Stanton and Alice were assessing their situation, desperate to start trying to find the answers to all of the symbols, codes and words they had found. Alice and Barney had now decided to place all their notes and findings on the floor around them. The sea of papers ruffled in a passing breeze.

"Barney, do you think we are ever going to find an answer? Are we ever going to know what this has all been about? What do you think, Barney?"

Jasper and Mrs Stanton had decided to sit down on the ground and join in with what Alice and Barney were doing.

Back part way down the tunnel Ms Pemberton had tripped, jettisoning the contents of her bag across the floor. Scrabbling around in the dirt she struggled to pick up all the items that now lay strewn across the uneven floor.

Placing her hand down to retrieve what she thought was a piece of white paper; Ms Pemberton noticed that it was in fact an envelope. The following words were scrawled and childlike:

‘ *Ms Pemberton*’

Intrigued, she paused to see what the envelope contained. Carefully opening the envelope up, she slowly removed the contents. Written on a scruffy piece of crumpled A4 paper were the following words:

*Dear Ms Pemberton,*

*I think about you often, and I am truly grateful to have you as my friend.*

*Thank you for being my rock, for sheltering me from the troubles we've both been through.*

*I cannot thank you enough and I have decided to write a poem for you here to try to explain how I feel about you.*

Ms Pemberton took a sudden step back; she had not realised how Barney had felt about her, or their friendship. She remembered how she had been rude to him on the village green that day.

Reading on, she now sat against the tunnel wall to read the poem that Barney had written:

*I Love You*

*You are beautiful*
*The scent of a summers' day*
*The warmth of the sun*
*Lay by my side, in the dewy grass and let us drift away.*

*Let me hold your hand*
*Let me guide your footsteps, with gentle love.*

*For you are my beautiful*
*My one true love.*

Ms Pemberton sat in silence, tears welling up and trying to force themselves out through her closed eyes. She now felt that all that they had been through had not been for nothing. Standing to her feet and now determined to find Barney and to make amends, Ms Pemberton hurriedly stuffed the remaining items she had dropped into her bag.

To save time and to make faster progress, she had also broken the heels off her stilettos, which would enable her to have an easier journey. Gathering speed and feeling charged by the letter and poem from Barney, Ms Pemberton strode forward with a renewed vigour and drive.

Barney, Alice, Jasper and Mrs Stanton were perusing the book and map. Jasper spoke saying, "Barney, Alice, look there—there it is!"

Barney and Alice looked at where Jasper had been pointing and wondered why he was getting so excited.

"What is it, Jasper old man? What have you spotted that our young eyes have not managed to find? Please do enlighten us; after all, we have been looking for quite some time."

Barney seemed miffed and annoyed that whatever Jasper had found had not been his discovery. "Come on then, Jasper – spill the beans. Tell us both what it is you think you've found."

Ms Pemberton was now almost as close as spitting distance to where Barney, Alice, Jasper and Mrs Stanton were sitting. Panting hard and trying to catch her breath Ms Pemberton could now see people ahead of her. Calling out she said, "Hello, up there. Can you tell me if there is a way out of here back to the village of Oakley Place?"

There appeared to be no response.

Barney and Alice thought they'd both heard something in the tunnel; it had sounded as if there was someone calling out. Looking at Mrs Stanton and Jasper who were both now engrossed in what Jasper had found, Barney and

Alice got to their feet. Jasper looked at them both in surprise, "Barney, Alice, where are you both sneaking off to? Come on, Barney, don't be a spoilsport. I promise I'll let you find it if it makes you both feel any better. I was just trying to help. You know, do my part…"

Barney and Alice were now both rushing towards the sound of someone out of breath coming towards them. Stopping for a moment to catch his breath, Barney came to a sudden halt. Blinking in the light, which was now growing strangely brighter, he could see a female moving closer towards him and Alice. Ms Pemberton could now see Barney perfectly clearly, and he too now saw that it was Ms Pemberton.

Both smiled a knowing smile, at the joy of finally being reunited together again.

# Chapter Twenty-Six
# Trust Me

In the tunnel, Barney and Ms Pemberton now embraced delighted to have been reunited. Both had resumed conversations, as if they had previously temporarily broken off mid-flow.

Alice stood watching as the two laughed in each other's company. As she stood there, Alice thought, *I wonder why Barney doesn't look at me like that. If only he would.*

Barney said, "Alice, do you remember Ms Pemberton from way back when we were in the sea of bodies?"

Alice looked confused, as if she had no idea what he was rambling on about. Shrugging her shoulders she said, "Sorry, Barney, I don't know what on earth you're talking about. Have you gone mad or something? Stuff it; I've had enough of you and Ms La-di-da there. I'm going back to Mrs Stanton and Jasper. At least I might get more sense out of the pair of them."

Alice stomped off back towards Jasper and Mrs Stanton.

Barney smiled at Ms Pemberton, "Alice, she's a funny one that one. I think she may be jealous of you, Ms Pemberton. Daft bat probably thinks there's something going on between the two of us, eh?"

Ms Pemberton looked as if she was about to speak; only after Barney's little comment about Alice she sensed that there was something going on between the two of them. They both walked quietly along the tunnel towards the others, neither knowing what the other one was secretly thinking and hoping, although Ms Pemberton knew she may be out of luck due to being years ahead of Barney.

Barney walked ahead and approached Jasper, Mrs Stanton and a grumpy-looking Alice, "Look who I have here – Jasper, Mrs Stanton, do you remember who she is? It's Ms Pemberton. You remember, the Parish Clerk of Oakley Place. She came looking to let you know that it seems that Frederick de Soames is no more."

Ms Pemberton leaned in to Barney and whispered, "I didn't come to tell you all about Frederick de Soames at all and how would I know that?"

Taking a step forward Ms Pemberton spoke, "Yes, Frederick de Soames is finally no more – his demise was swift according to our sources."

Jasper, Mrs Stanton and Alice all looked puzzled. In unison they said, "But how can that be?"

Jasper looked at Barney and Ms Pemberton. "When did this happen? Do you know when?"

Looking now at Mrs Stanton, Jasper had a sudden realisation: had Frederick de Soames met his death on that day of revelation when all time and space had changed?

Barney and Alice had started to pack the book and map back into their bags. Barney looked up, "Alice, I wonder what happened to him, I mean really happened. What source do you think she was talking about?"

Alice glared at Barney.

Ms Pemberton was leaning over them as they continued to pack away the book, papers and map.

Alice whispered, "She gives me the heebie-jeebies, that one. Why do you think she keeps glaring at me like that?"

Barney did not respond to Alice's comments. He just smiled and carried on with what he had been doing.

Jasper looked around at Ms Pemberton, "So, how are you, my dear? You're looking very well. Oh yes, you're

Martin Fothergill's girlfriend, aren't you?"

Ms Pemberton squirmed.

She had realised that was how the villagers in Oakley Place had thought of her. Not wanting to be rude or stand-offish Ms Pemberton said, "Oh, me and Martin Fothergill, we're just close friends really. He was married although his wife lived overseas. Yes, we…we're just good friends, that's all."

Ms Pemberton had now moved and crouched down next to Barney, hoping that he would shield her from further invasive questions.

Barney felt Ms Pemberton moving closer, "Are you okay, Ms Pemberton? You seem to be a bit twittered."

Ms Pemberton turned towards him and whispered, "I just wish people wouldn't keep asking me about Martin Fothergill. Trust me; it was no bed of roses. He was not the mild-mannered gent that he tried to portray. Even though his wife was not here, she seemed to be the dominant party. Martin was always adding to his little entourage of women and I was just one in a long line of many, you see, Barney. Do you remember that day when we met on the High Street and I pushed a note and the talisman into your hand? Did you read what I had put in the note?"

Barney recoiled on his heels, as if he had been hit right between his eyes. "Ms Pemberton, are you trying to tell me that you like me or is there something more to all this? Can you remember what the note said?"

Alice, Mrs Stanton and Jasper were all starting off back down the tunnel heading back towards the cellar and normality. Ms Pemberton and Barney gazed into each other's eyes trying to reach each other's souls.

Looking up, Barney noticed that Alice, Jasper and Mrs Stanton had started off down the tunnel without them. Barney shouted after them, "Oi, you lot! Where do you think you're all going without us then, marching off? Wait up! We'll catch up in a moment."

Ms Pemberton was starting to stand up. She paused again and said, "Barney, do you think we could ever …you know …be more than just good friends?"

Barney smiled a wry smile and said, "I don't know, Ms Pemberton. Let's just wait and see. Come on, we've got to catch that lot up. I'll be blown if I'll let Alice get back before me."

Ms Pemberton followed Barney a few steps behind, as he was going at full pelt trying to catch up with Alice, Jasper and Mrs Stanton.

He shouted after them all, "Come on you slow coaches, I'll be back before you all if you're not careful. A snail would be faster than the pace you're all going."

Barney, Ms Pemberton, Alice, Jasper and Mrs Stanton were now all back at the opening of the cellar at Jasper's house. They were all busily trying to squeeze through the opening. Once through the hole they fumbled and groped their way through the darkness in the cellar.

Mrs Stanton said, "Jasper love, when things have settled down do you think we could get the light fixed in here? I'm not enjoying this experience one bit. What I need right now is a nice cup of tea and a lovely slice of chocolate cake. Does anyone fancy joining me when we've all had a chance to sort ourselves out? You know, have a wee and a brush up."

She nudged Barney and Jasper and giggled like a naughty schoolgirl.

Before they had stepped through from the cellar into the hallway Ms Pemberton paused, "Jasper, Mrs Stanton and Barney, I should probably tell you about two men that entered your house a day or so ago. They broke in and appeared to have been looking for something in Barney's room first of all and then rampaged through downstairs. I sneaked in while they were both upstairs. I don't think they noticed me. Then when I found the opening, I thought, well, there might have been a secret way out into Oakley Place. Sadly I didn't find one though. I did find all of you, which was the best part."

They had now all arrived and were standing in the hallway of Jasper and Mrs Stanton's house.

# Chapter Twenty-Seven
# Hope

Barney had stashed all of the food and water that Alice had brought him into his rucksack, which strained under the weight of the bulging contents. He made his way out through the gap he and Alice had clambered through before and headed back out into the tunnel passageway. The darkness was clinging to him — he'd found some matches and a stack of candles, along with the old lantern, which was battered and worn, but somehow still fully functioning. Taking the book and map out of his rucksack he tried to find somewhere that was not cold or damp.

There was a sudden draught, similar to when a window is opened on a blustery day. The air rushed by, rustling the pages and blowing the map further down the tunnel. Barney tried to catch it while attempting to stop the book from falling and the candles from blowing out.

He had lined a row of candles up against the wall; water dripped down from the ceiling of the tunnel, but somehow missed the flickering flames as they bobbed and weaved patterns across the walls. Barney managed to catch hold of the map before it could once again flip free, and continue on its way. Pinning the map firmly under the weight of the rucksack he now sat and pondered what he would do.

Thinking aloud to himself, he said, '*Wow! That was a lucky escape – I don't know what or where I'd be now without good old Jasper, Alice and Mrs Stanton.*'

He once again flitted in to an altered state and started to mutter to himself – he did this every time something had got under his skin; it seemed to send his circuitry haywire. Hope balanced thick in the air like indigestible soup. Looking through the book and his notes he tried to decipher another clue; he had noticed a few more codes and symbols along the tunnel walls and felt sure that if he just kept chipping away he would solve this code and get the answers they had all waited so long for. The candles danced like jumping sprites, taking flight on a moonlit night.

After what had been a good hour or two, he heard footsteps coming towards him. He hastily moved the map and put the book and notes under the rucksack, then propped himself up against them all.

"Barney, we made it at last! I told you I would be back, didn't I, lad? I've brought Alice with me too and well, Mrs Stanton insisted on coming back with us too. She's packed enough blooming food to feed an army and then some."

Barney seemed to perk up; he at least managed a smile, albeit brief.

"Where have you been? I thought you were just gonna leave me here and forget about me. Mind you, I wouldn't blame you if you did – it's probably what I deserve. What must you think of me, not wanting to go with my parents like that? Well, have they gone? Have they?"

Barney seemed excited and exuberant at the thought that his parents would no longer be in his life. "So, what did you do with them? Bump them off, Jasper, and bury their bodies under the rhubarb, did we Jasper?"

Jasper, Alice and Mrs Stanton looked alarmed.

"Barney Lumsden, how can you be so wicked boy, and about such lovely parents as you've got?" said Mrs Stanton, oblivious to Barney's past history.

Jasper butted in, "So, Barney lad, what have you been up to while you've been waiting? How's it going solving those riddles and clues you and Alice have found?"

Looking at the scribbled notes, Jasper deduced that Barney had been working on trying to make a start on solving the clues and deciphering the codes.

Engrossed in the book and scrutinising what was written, Barney looked up and said, "Jasper, I'm glad you're here now, I may need your help. Can I ask you some questions, please?"

Jasper plonked himself down next to Barney. "What would you like to know, Barney lad?"

Getting out his notebook and pen Barney sat primed to write down the answers. Looking into Jasper's eyes he said, "So, Jasper, about how long have you lived in Oakley Place? What do you know about the Curtain Twitchers? Who is Frederick de Soames and why is he coming back?"

Eyes closed, Jasper was now in a contemplative state, his mind searching for answers to the bombardment of questions issued by Barney.

His eyes suddenly sprang open and stared at Barney, "Right then, where to start. I guess at the beginning would be as good a place as any. Well, Mrs Stanton and I have lived in Oakley for many lifetimes it seems. Born and bred here, the pair of us. The Curtain Twitchers, you ask – that's a whole lifetime's worth of explanation – not sure where to begin with that one, lad, really. As you may have heard, or read, the Curtain Twitchers are like the guardians of Oakley Place. They've always been here since I don't quite know when – I think most definitely since there had been the plague here in Oakley Place, whenever that was? That I'm sorry to say I cannot tell you, Barney. Yes, yes! Frederick de Soames – I can tell you all about that despicable character – heart as black as coal that one – that's if he indeed has a heart in that soulless body of his. Right, Barney, has that little bit of knowledge helped you at all?"

Barney was still scribbling, his hand frantically writing every little word down as if his life depended on it. "Yes, Jasper, there was one last question I think you may have forgotten to answer: that was the one about when Frederick de Soames is meant to be coming back? Don't suppose that the Major said anything? I can't remember."

Jasper looked blankly at Barney. "But you were there, Barney. You heard everything, don't you remember? You even asked again, even though the Major must have said it at least a dozen or more times. I thought my memory was bad!"

Barney was annoyed with Jasper's comment. He edged away and tried to carry on attempting to decipher the symbols and codes with Alice. Mrs Stanton was pouring out some tea from a flask, and had arranged some food on plates.

"Here you go, Jasper. Have a brew, you must be parched – this dust down here really sticks in your throat, doesn't it? How about some food? There are a few of your favourite sandwiches and a lovely cream scone. Barney, Alice, would you both like some too?"

Barney and Alice glanced around to see Mrs Stanton awkwardly juggling cups and plates. Dashing across, Alice attempted to catch the wobbling cups from her hands.

"Thank you, Alice, you are a sweet girl. Barney, you've got a good one there so you have. Keep hold of her for as long as you can. Girls like that are like pure gold!"

Alice blushed and looked embarrassed.

Barney turned around, "Yes, she's a diamond – I'm not sure I would be here still if it wasn't for Alice."

Alice now looked like a bright red beetroot; she was positively glowing in their admiration. Jasper, Mrs Stanton, Barney and Alice had enjoyed time together – if that had been at all possible in a dank dark tunnel. All was calm, all was quiet and all was bliss.

# Chapter Twenty-Eight
# The Wise Ones

Jasper and Mrs Stanton had been, and would always remain, in Oakley Place until the demise of Frederick de Soames. Since the arrival of Frederick de Soames in Oakley Place their lives and destinies had been sealed. They had learned their wise ways from their ancestors who had passed on their knowledge, wisdom and ancient practices through time.

From the very breath of mankind the Wise Ones had been entrusted to find the solution and return to the ways of love and the deliverance from darkness.

Jasper and Mrs Stanton had also nursed those who had been blighted with the plague. Those that had partially recovered from the plague had been bringing hope through ancient herbal cures. At the time the plague had arrived in Oakley Place, many Wise Ones had been accused of witchcraft and the dark arts. Jasper and Mrs Stanton, or Sarah Seagrove as she was known then, had both fled the 'Witch Finder Generals' who had wrongly brought many Wise Ones to an untimely death.

They lived by ancient ways, which many people did not understand and consequently so many people thought they were in league with the devil himself and were therefore witches. So many innocents were killed simply for being true to who they were.

Mrs Stanton and Jasper had run from village to village until they had found the shelter of Oakley Place. Well hidden, the village was buried deep within the depths of a deep wooded enclave. The village named 'Oakley Place' had not always had the name and had previously been known as just 'Oakley'. The 'Place' had been added just shortly after World War II. No one ever found out why; that was just what had been decided at the time.

Oakley back in the 1340s had been a tiny place hidden in the woods amongst the great mighty Oaks and Limes. The village had grown from a ramshackle collection of a higgledy-piggledy quarry workers' huts through clearings in the woods to the newly expanding growth of a developing village as it had become today.

To Jasper and Mrs Stanton it had been the perfect place for them both to hide, and it had been a veritable sea of natural herbal treasures for the potions and treatments they made for the villagers back then.

"Jasper, 'tis time to find wild sage and thyme to make nosegays for the poor souls at death's dark door. For the smell of death hangs heavy in the air", Barney joked in a silly voice that Mrs Stanton had said this according to what Jasper had told him.

Putting on a serious tone, Barney continued to tell Alice about Jasper and Mrs Stanton.

"Sarah Seagrove had travelled with Jasper through many lifetimes. It was in October 1914, shortly after the battle had started in Ypres that Sarah Seagrove had met First Officer Stanton. He had been a dashing chap with a happy demeanour considering the brutalities of war that he had witnessed on those killing fields. Sarah had been the nurse he had been brought to in the makeshift field hospital after suffering a serious injury. It was a quick fix place and once the injured had been patched up they were sent back to the battlefield, there was no time for compassion and kindness. On this occasion it was going to be a few more days for First Officer Stanton; it was love at first sight between the two of them. Time was short and in the heat of the moment they had decided to be together.

They were married within a matter of a few short days, and prior to First Officer Stanton being sent back to play his part in battle, which was to honour his commitment to 'King and Country' after some disparagement and discord. First Officer Stanton was quickly redeployed back to the frontline. Apparently Jasper had been there too. Luckily Jasper had survived in one piece, but First Officer Stanton never returned from the battlefield. After the war Mrs Stanton and Jasper found each other again, and things just picked up from where they had been left, as if they had never been apart. From that day forward they've never been apart, and even if they do drift, it's usually not for long. Mrs Stanton never did really recover after that and she vowed that she'd never find love again."

Barney sat talking to Alice out in the garden of Jasper and Mrs Stanton's house, as they both enjoyed the smells and sounds of summer. Barney had been talking to Alice about how Jasper and Mrs Stanton had met. He'd been talking for the best part of the afternoon. Alice was trying to keep herself awake by eating Jelly Babies and Chocolate Buttons that had melted in the afternoon sun.

"A little bonkers really, isn't it, Barney?" Alice remarked as she flicked through her notebook. "I suppose it is but it's all starting to make sense now…I think?"

Barney looked as if he had started to fit all the pieces together like a giant jigsaw puzzle.

"Oh my goodness, Alice, I've just remembered something that happened. Do you remember I told you how I'd been out on the street that first time? Well, when I was sleeping rough out on the filth-filled streets, just lying on my bit of cardboard and trying to shelter from the rain, I had decided to thumb through one of the books from the library. In the morning I made my excuses to Jimmy, the homeless man who'd helped me out overnight and kept me safe from the drug pushers and pimps. In the morning I headed off to find the public toilets to have a quick wash and sort myself out. I then made a dash for it to get to the library in time for the talk. Damn it! Alice, that's where I had met Jasper before."

Barney was elated, and had proceeded to do a happy dance. Alice looked startled; she had been lost in her own thoughts and had not really been taking any notice of anything Barney had been talking to her about.

"Sorry, Barney, what was that? You were saying?"

Barney started again, "Remember I'd said about this talk I went to about alternative realities, quantum leaping and what was it he said…something about what your thoughts becoming real or something like that?"

Barney frowned at Alice.

Fidgeting, Alice tried to appear interested, even though she was not really bothered about a word Barney had said most of the afternoon. Sitting still for a few moments she smiled, "Yes, Barney, I think I do. Anyway, carry on…I am all ears now."

In an excited tone Barney jumped in all guns blazing, "Well, the man was Jasper – it was him all right. We all had a cuppa and he chatted after the talk with Mrs Turnball, my teacher from school who had rocked up to offer moral support, and he also chatted to me. He was quite weird, thinking about it, in a funny, odd way. I didn't really think too much about it at the time. I just thought that's how enlightened folk were and left it at that. Now coming to think of it, I remember him saying at the end: I'm sure we'll meet again. At the time I thought, woo that's a bit odd. After that I guess I never remembered meeting Jasper, it didn't even register in my head, even on that night at the back of the old Government buildings."

Barney sat trying to figure out this bolt out of the blue, and digest the monumental life-changing discovery about Jasper and Mrs Stanton. From that moment on he knew that nothing would ever be the same again, here in Oakley Place. He also understood why he had always felt so many times after that talk at the library as if something or someone had been watching over him; maybe they had been watching and protecting him. And what if it had been the Twitchers or the Wise Ones?

Alice and Barney stopped talking about Jasper and Mrs Stanton.

"Barney, are you okay? You're acting a bit weird, even for you."

Barney snapped out of his deep thought and jolted back into the here and now with Alice. "So Alice, did you find anything else out when you were digging about?"

Alice had now glazed over and was looking a bit vacant, "No, I don't think so – I may head off tomorrow or later to see what I can find in the local library about 'Wise Ones' and the 'Twitchers'. Thanks for bringing me up to speed on your little chat with Jasper. It was fascinating."

Alice grimaced, as if to say it was as boring as watching paint dry.

"Okay Alice, you need to go then. Won't the local library in the next village be closing soon?"

Alice checked her shabby chic watch, "Yes, I suppose I best get going. I'll be seeing you, Barney."

She shuffled off out of Jasper's front door, and gave Barney a cheeky wink as she left.

Barney disappeared upstairs to his bedroom, and watched Alice as she walked across the village green towards the bus stop. He thought to himself, *'She's totally nuts, that girl. I really don't get why she's so seemingly interested, when most of the time it's as if she isn't really listening to me at all.'*

While looking out of his bedroom window, he spotted Ms Pemberton chatting to Jasper and Mrs Stanton, who had been out on their daily walk around the village, which they seemed to do every day.

Almost as if they had been checking everything was in its place, so to speak. Ms Pemberton looked up towards the window. I dipped out the way just in case she thought I was a Twitcher. Jasper and Mrs Stanton were out there for quite a while. They never did say what they'd all been talking about. It was probably something and nothing. I certainly wasn't going to worry my head about it. I sat down on the floor and started flicking through the papers. The pile did seem lighter but maybe Jasper had thrown a few on to stoke the fire. It was too late now and for whatever reason he'd done it, I'm sure Jasper would have had a perfectly good reason. For all I knew it was most likely for the best. After all, these things usually are, aren't they?

Mrs Stanton and Jasper came through the front door, taking off their coats and slipping on their cosy slippers.

Jasper shouted, "Barney, are you up there? We're back from our walk now. Are you joining Mrs Stanton and I for tea? She's just off now to get tea started, should be ready soon."

There was no response from Barney.

Jasper shrugged his shoulders, and proceeded into the parlour to cosy up by the open fire. He was still feeling a chill and wanted to make sure he was not going to be laid low with the flu or a summer cold. These things did happen.

Mrs Stanton, meanwhile, was happy in her own little world, creating a meal fit for a king in the kitchen at the back of the house.

Barney was busy listening to his iPod in his bedroom and happily getting down to some beats, while reading through the Government papers. About half an hour later Barney surfaced from his bedroom, ravenous. Ambling downstairs and into the parlour he asked, "So what's for tea tonight, Mrs Stanton?" and gave her a cheeky smile.

Taken aback Mrs Stanton mumbled, "Hog's head and Pease pudding, followed by damsons and plums. I have also made some homemade sweet mead."

Barney screwed his face up at the very thought. Even just saying the words made him want to throw up.

Jasper and Mrs Stanton started to laugh, "Oh Barney, you're so gullible! Don't panic, lad, we're not eating that tonight. But we are having fish and chips, your favourite, right Barney? Followed by a nice homemade apple pie and cream. I've even pushed the boat out and brought a bottle of fizzy pop, not sure which, Tango or Pepsi."

Barney looked relieved and sat down at the table. Mrs Stanton and Jasper both went to bring the food in to eat on trays in the parlour. Jasper laughed, "We thought that would get you going, Barney. Although that is one of our favourite dishes from the old times."

Jasper and Barney looked at each other in a knowing way across the room while they were eating tea. Each wanted to ask the other a question about the missing pages and papers, but neither ever did that afternoon. Nor did they at any time after that day.

Barney kept the remaining pages and papers safely hidden from prying eyes and out of Jasper's reach. Barney decided that would be for the best, just in case Jasper took it into his head to burn the rest of the pages and papers, in his attempt to cover up the Government's involvement, or in his efforts to protect the 'Wise Ones' and the 'Twitchers'.

# Chapter Twenty-Nine
# The Government: Cover-up

Major Buttertone-Smithe sat in his office hidden away from prying eyes; he was not as upfront or as honest as he had led everyone to believe. Books were stacked neatly around his pristine office, which was situated in the heart of London. Walls of panelled oak, which had been polished to perfection, surrounded him on every side. The heaviness of the oak panelling, acted as an encasement for him to hide within all of his secrets and lies.

On a small table in the centre of the spacious room, sat an unopened file. Written on the outside it stated **'Confidential'** in large red overpowering letters. Then directly underneath this neat alignment of a word was scrawled, **'Oakley Place'** as though it had been an afterthought hastily added by the Major.

Jasper sat in the parlour talking to Barney.

"Major Buttertone-Smithe has only been a resident in Oakley Place for ten to twelve years. Prior to this he had been seen about the village at various events like the annual village fete, and at the time there had been an elderly lady who everyone naturally presumed was his aunt."

Barney, now sat captivated by Jasper, and was trying to piece the last strands of the jig-saw together.

"So what else do you know about Major Buttertone-Smithe, Jasper?"

Pausing, Jasper tried to think clearly so that he could give Barney all the bare facts. He didn't want to tell him absolutely everything though, just enough to keep him guessing for now. The rest, after all, would appear as if by magic!

Plumping himself up, and readjusting his position in his favourite chair near the open fire, he pondered trying to formulate the right words to say that may sit easily on the young lad's shoulders, and would not give Barney sleepless nights thinking about what had been said.

Jasper thought, *'Barney, poor lad's been through enough in his young life already and most likely seen more than his fair share of darkness than anyone could have stomached in a lifetime.'*

"Right, Barney, here's what I can tell you as there are certain things that I'm not at liberty to tell you due to the Official Secrets Act that us Government employees have had to sign as part of the deal with the job. I hope you understand?"

Barney had been writing everything down, although his book was now nearly full with scribblings and code-cracking, prospective answers ran alongside poems he had penned. He just loved to write; it was like an escape where he could just be 'Barney'.

"So go on, Jasper, spill the beans, what else can you tell me? Do you know what these papers are all about?"

Jasper looked intrigued as Barney pulled the papers out from beneath his notebook for the first time. The papers were a little creased and dog-eared. Some of the loose pages looked as if they had come from an old file. Others had 'Confidential Property of the Government' stamped across them in bright red ink. A couple of pages were also the worse for wear, with what looked like coffee stains as if they had been used to mop up a spill at some time. Barney and Jasper now moved from their comfortable seats, and placed the papers across the old table in the parlour. They slowly scanned each page, their eyes intensely digesting each word and letter to see if it threw up any answers or clues.

"Barney, where did you get this lot from? There's a lot of stuff here that, shall we just say, if the Government knew it had fallen into your hands there could be all kinds of implications. Are these the papers from that night when I caught you outside the old Government building that I had been patrolling?"

Barney was engrossed; he'd spotted something written about Banthom's Biological Laboratory.

In excitement, Barney looked at Jasper, "LOOK! Can you see, Jasper? There it is: Banthom's Biological Laboratory, and look, Jasper, there are letters between Major Buttertone-Smithe and the lab."

Jasper had now grabbed his glasses and started reading the pages intently, soaking up each word and sentence.

"I see what you mean, Barney – Banthom's Biological Laboratory. Isn't that the place you were taken to, Barney? Didn't you say they were making some kind of antidote?"

As they both read on it became a lot more apparent that the whole set-up was more sinister than they had at first thought: Major Buttertone-Smithe had at some point crossed paths with Frederick de Soames.

Sadly this is where the well seems to run dry.

*' I popped back up to my bedroom to check the holdall, as I thought some pages were missing, and to stop my brain working overtime. I thought it best to just check one last time that I had definitely got everything from inside the holdall.'*

Now heading up the stairs to his bedroom, Barney shouted to Jasper, who was in the parlour rifling through the papers.

Barney called out, "Jasper, I'm just going to make sure I've not left any more of the papers – I think I may have left something in the holdall. I'll be back in a few minutes. Why don't you carry on looking to see if you can spot anything else?"

There was silence from Jasper, who had indeed spotted something else on more than one of the papers: he had found the results of the tests that the Major had been doing on the residents of Oakley Place for years without anyone suspecting anything at all. It appeared that Bathom's Biological Laboratory, had been in the background processing the results. There were also a few papers about Jasper and Mrs Stanton. Jasper did not like what he was reading one bit. He continued reading each page; each page was more damning than the one before. Jasper knew that if Barney had seen the pages, let's just say if he had, he would be making a run for it. And the rest would have been history.

Jasper was now in deep contemplation about what he should do next, *'I can't let that happen. That would be like signing all our death warrants in one fell swoop. I know I'll quickly find the firelighter and light a fire in the sooty hearth. I'll shout up to Barney not to hurry. He's still not down so I'll start throwing the discriminating papers onto the fire. Not all of them, just the ones that would cause the most damage. After all, I'm getting pretty good at damage limitation these days. The Government has also been a watchful presence on mine and Mrs Stanton's lives for centuries but we never knew quite why. However, now I think I do?'*

Barney returned out of breath, "Are you okay, Jasper? Feeling a bit chilly? Why have you lit a fire? It's the middle of summer for goodness' sake – it's like a flipping oven in here. I'll be down to my boxer shorts if we don't get some air in here, Jasper!"

Barney had taken off his lightweight hoody, and was starting to drip with sweat.

Jasper tried to act normally and pulled on his cardigan, which had been draped over the back of his chair.

"Oh yes, I lit the fire because I think I may be coming down with a cold or the flu, Barney. Us old folks have to be careful at our age. I suddenly got a chill, and thought, oh no, I'm not having that. So I just lit the fire for just a little while. I'll put it out once I've warmed up. Barney, I'm just nipping off to see how Mrs Stanton is getting on in the kitchen, she's making some of her homemade chicken soup and we'll also have a chunk of her lovely homemade crusty bread – that should soon sort me out. Back in a few minutes, lad."

Jasper started to head towards the kitchen; he slowed his pace and looked back into the parlour to check what Barney was doing. As he did he shouted, "Oh, Barney, did you find what you were looking for upstairs in your bedroom?"

He waited to see what Barney's reaction would be and what he may have been doing. He was met once again with silence. Barney had his iPod on and was flicking through the loose pages on the table, in his own little world. Barney looked at the table. When he had arrived back in the room there didn't seem to be any difference to the number of papers he had left on the table before going upstairs. It was then that he noticed some papers burning in the fireplace. Looking a little closer he spotted what looked like the corner of one of the Government papers, but by the time he realised and had tried to pull it out of the fireplace, it had shrivelled in the flames and disappeared without a trace.

Barney could now hear Jasper and Mrs Stanton chatting, on their way back towards the parlour. Quickly Barney gathered all of the remaining pages and papers together, and hid them under some magazines as fast as he could. He wondered if Jasper had thrown some onto the fire. But why would he have done that?

Mrs Stanton and Jasper came ambling into the parlour, tottering along with a tray of bread and chicken soup, and a tray laden with cake and tea. Sitting down now around the table the conversation changed and Barney realised that he may have just lost his only opportunity to ask Jasper any more questions. Although Barney had obviously missed his golden opportunity to find out what Jasper was hiding, he had at least discovered that the Government had been involved in all of the strange occurrences in 'Oakley Place' for centuries. Barney would now wait to see what else he would find, and try to dig a little as far as Jasper was concerned.

As they sat eating lunch, Jasper leaned forward towards Barney and said, "Some things are just not meant to be found, Barney, but that doesn't mean to say they're not right in front of your eyes."

Barney sat back in his chair confused.

*'What was that supposed to mean?'*

The conversation changed and Mrs Stanton had switched on the radio, which had lifted the sinking feeling in the room.

*'After all, of all the stuff Jasper had said during my time here in Oakley Place, that was probably one of the strangest comments he had ever made. I had even come to believe in all the stuff he had spoken about at that talk on alternate realities, and what he had said about thoughts becoming things, all those years ago with Mrs Turnball.'*

Jasper's comment now set me thinking, and I knew that tonight, would probably end up being a long night.

# Chapter Thirty

# The Seekers of Light and Truth

For a millennia there had always been seekers of truth, way beyond the confines of time and space.

Barney, had started his journey about the time his parents had stopped caring and had forgotten to uphold their promise and the deal of parenthood, which was to love and care for their child; in this case, Barney. At twelve years of age, and after being left again with his drunken aunt and his drug-addled uncle, he had decided that he would do anything and everything to make sure he would live a better life than this. After school Barney would visit the local library, read books and dream. Over the next three years he started to formulate a dream, a vision and a grand plan to escape the darkness all around him.

Barney sat in the New Age section at his local library. A poster on the entrance of the library stated:

*'Guest speaker, Jasper Swift, will be giving a talk on alternate realities and the 'Adventurers of Time and Space'. The talk starts at 11 a.m. Free: to all seekers of the truth.'*

Intrigued, Barney wrote a note on a page of his school homework book about the talk. While he was writing, thoughts started to mingle about the pros and cons of going to the talk.

*'There was no age restriction and as it was a weekend, there would be no one looking after me. My parents were usually creating an illusion of grandeur with some newly acquired rich influential friends in their ridiculous attempt to better themselves, even though things were not that great really. Hence that was why I ended up growing up so quick beyond my time. I picked up a couple of books by an amazing bloke named Mike Dooley who was an adventurer of Time and Space. One of the books I'd decided to take home was called 'Infinite Possibilities: The Art of Living Your Dreams', and the other was called 'Notes from the Universe: New Perspectives from an Old Friend'. Both mind-blowing, something resonated within me as I read each page within each of these books. I'd also recently watched a DVD at school in PSHE or RE called 'The Secret'. Mrs Turnball, our schoolteacher, was pretty cool – I think most of the time she'd try to teach us these alternative points of view. I'm sure it was against the school's new curriculum and I was certain that if*

*the old head teacher, Mr Pritchard, ever had inkling that she was teaching us this stuff he'd be throwing her out of school. Fortunately though for Mrs Turnball, she was the coolest teacher ever, and remarkably Mr Pritchard had not yet sussed what Mrs Turnball had been doing. Well, suppose I best get going. Who knows, mum and dad may be back.'*

Barney grabbed the books and booked them out with the self-service automated machine. A stern-looking matronly type librarian peered over her half-rim glasses, in a disapproving way. Barney smiled and headed out of the library.

He left the library and hopped onto the Tube. It was now only a few stops to where he lived in Alvanley Gardens, West Hampstead, in one of the big houses. This was one of the many perks of dad's job, although it was now starting to look a little tired. Signs were starting to show that they had taken a dive financially, as the house was becoming quite grimy.

When they'd first moved here they supposedly had a cleaner and a maid doing their bidding and keeping the place sparkling, ready to entertain their high-and-mighty friends. When money had started to evaporate and dad had slipped off the wagon, that was the beginning really. They sacked the maid and sent her packing and by now the cleaner only came when they were entertaining their friends, which was very rare these days.

I sat waiting, but there was no sign of them. I grabbed a few pieces of bread and cut off the mould and found a tin of tomato soup that had seen better days, the date only just out. I warmed it up on the cooker and sat down at the grubby kitchen table, dipping the bread in the soup to try to fill me up. After tea I decided to head up to my room. I shut the doors downstairs, but kept the light on as if pretending someone was in, just to deter any unwanted intruders.

We'd been done over before and they never did find out what went missing. Personally I think it was a scam by my parents so they could claim off the insurance. The reason I say that is because it was about a week after the payout arrived that they'd hotfooted it without me on a skiing trip to Switzerland. That time they left me with my Aunt Ruby, who actually was not too bad; at least she was caring and loved me. Sadly she died of breast cancer some months back, and mum never wanted to talk about her sister after the funeral. She'd always burst into tears.

Barney sat in his room flicking through the two books he had borrowed from the library, scanning each page, and scrutinising every line as if he was drinking in every word.

The wind rattled at the glass in his bedroom window and the howled menacingly, as it whipped around the outside of the house. The house was always full of creaks and strange noises, sometimes you could hear the faint sound of the bats up in the attic or mice scuttling under the old floorboards.

It was now approaching 2:00 a.m. and still no parents. Barney knew it would be another day of raiding his piggy bank, so he could scrape enough money to get something decent to eat for lunch at school. He got out of his school uniform, and folded it as neatly as he could, as it was the only clean school uniform that he had. Still, it was almost Friday and he'd have to try to wash it in the sink, as there had been a few red letters, about the electricity board coming to cut them off for non-payment.

He'd been getting by pretty well so far. Money was hidden here and there around the house, as mum had a secret stash in an old tea caddy, which was hidden at the back of a cupboard. She had called it her rainy day fund, and had made so many promises to Barney of the things they would do, but none of them ever happened. Each dream had been shattered and gone up in smoke long ago.

Gathering his things together and rushing to get himself ready for school Barney brushed his hair and headed for the kitchen. He drank the last dregs of milk and found some stale cream crackers. Not the greatest of breakfasts, but at least it was better than nothing. Heading off to school, Barney started to plan his trip to the library the following day.

His school day passed and it was almost time to head off. Last lesson of the day was with Mrs Turnball. As he was packing his bag, one of the books he had picked up from the library slipped out, and landed with a thud on the floor. Mrs Turnball turned and bent down to pick up the book from the floor.

Handing the book back to Barney she said, "Barney, is everything okay at home? Sorry, here's your book, you must have dropped it out of your bag – looks interesting. Good choice, Mike Dooley's 'Infinite Possibilities'. Did you know there's a talk on at the library tomorrow? I may go if you fancy joining me, Barney?"

Barney took the book from Mrs Turnball, and quickly put it back in his bag, feeling a little embarrassed at first. Mrs Turnball went back to get her things together. As Barney left the classroom, he paused and said, "Miss, did you really mean you'd be happy for me to join you at the talk tomorrow? I would like to go but I just feel well, you know, a bit odd. A young kid going to something like that – it's really unusual, isn't it?"

Mrs Turnball smiled and said, "I'll meet you in the coffee shop next door to the library and we can go together. I felt a bit nervous the first time I went to one of these talks. See you tomorrow then, Barney."

That evening, Barney got back home to find his parents quarrelling again; they hadn't even noticed him coming through the front door. Barney felt himself crumple inside; that would have been it really, the talk tomorrow would have been a definite no. Harriett Lumsden, Barney's mother, was dressed in her designer suit downing a glass of Prosecco and his father, Jeremy Lumsden, looked a little worse for wear, flicking through a copy of *The Times*.

Jeremy Lumsden looked up suddenly, "Harriett, did you hear something or was that the wind?"

Harriett turned and glanced Barney starting to walk upstairs to his room. Joking she said, "Oh, it's only Barney squirrelling off up to his room. Disgraceful really, you'd think he'd at least want to see his mum and dad, wouldn't you? I mean, it's not as if he sees us every day. Damn rude if you ask me. Jeremy love, get the little oik to come downstairs to see his lovely mummy, will you, please?"

Jeremy Lumsden always did his wife Harriett's bidding. He pounded upstairs and burst into Barney's room, grabbing him and catching him with a right hook, sending

Barney crashing to the floor. Jeremy Lumsden had no feelings for Barney, since the death of his dear little Charlotte, Barney's half-sister, who he'd never even met.

Barney whimpered, and tried to move out of his way.

Grabbing his bag and the book he had been reading, he stumbled downstairs slightly bloodied, and ran out of the front door banging it hard behind him.

He could hear his oh-so-loving parents again, having yet another blazing row.

This was his first of many nights out on the street. As he had said he was going to the talk at the library, Barney decided to head in that direction. He had noticed a few homeless folk and there was one in particular, who he had chatted to now and again. Maybe he could pitch with this homeless bloke for tonight. After all, it would probably most likely, only be for one night. He could go home tomorrow; his parents wouldn't be there anyway. They never were at weekends, as it was, they had most likely only gone home to pick up fresh clothes anyway.

That night Barney slept on the street. At least it was safer than being at home.

*'Feeling empty and bloodied, I found a few pieces of cardboard to use as a bed during the night out here on the street. One of the homeless folk that I had chatted to previously let me bed down near him. At least I'll have a bit of warmth and protection especially as he's pretty streetwise, and I'm not that streetwise yet. Tomorrow I would find some of the answers, I hoped and maybe I could start my journey away from this hell that had been my life so far. Who knows, maybe I'd even get one or two dreams and a great big dollop of love thrown into the bargain. I can but hope, but for now tonight I just wanted to sleep and tomorrow would be the first step to a new start. I hoped, and dreamed at least that would be true.'*

# Chapter Thirty-One
# The Answer is: LOVE

Back now on the village green in Oakley Place, all five stood unified and strong in the changing circle of life that was being born into reality. A common bond now joined them all. It had always been there and was indeed the answer to all their searching. For the answer to all their journeys was 'LOVE'.

Jasper said to Barney, Alice and Ms Pemberton, "The code was deciphered through all your thoughts, feelings and dreams that you've all experienced while reading this book. The truth and the answers were there within your grasp all along, just waiting for you to find it within your own hearts and minds. To manifest and create the answer that would only come when you all believed, trusted and opened your hearts to each other, which in turn cracked the code of the 'Curtain Twitchers' and revealed the answer."

Love for each other, the love through time and most importantly of all, the love in all hearts past, present, and in the future of an evolving world.

Scanning through the pages, it became clear to them all, that the answer had always been right in front of their blinkered eyes.

Barney, Alice, Ms Pemberton, Jasper and Mrs Stanton now understood why they had all been brought together as one: love bound them in this journey and would also now carry them forward into a new dawn. Life for them all would never be the same again. A light switch of realisation had finally been pushed, releasing them from all doubt and dark looming fears. Emotions were now high, as they started to travel back into the light of Oakley Place.

Nothing now seemed to matter as long as they had each other. All five of them had been through so much together, and on they would now go as one into a new adventure. The death of Frederick de Soames had been the catalyst of a seismic shift, which had altered reality and all dimensions right across time and space. Everything that had passed had been rewritten into the future. The end was now rewinding like an old cassette tape, taking them back to the beginning and creating a whole new world.

Ms Pemberton and Alice now understood their relationship with Barney, but neither dared admit it. Barney was definitely not into the whole relationship deal and thought his entanglements with either of them, would have been just passing fads. By being remote and aloof he could keep them both as friends, and for now that would be better than not having either in his life.

Jasper and Mrs Stanton were now relieved to be back and overjoyed that the nightmare had come to an end.

Jasper said, "We'll be able to begin a whole new life now that the curse of Frederick de Soames has been lifted from our lives. I'm looking forward to enjoying happy times, until our days end."

Laughing, Barney, Alice and Ms Pemberton said, "What a difference there is now. Everything is brighter and the atmosphere in Oakley Place seems to have lifted. Look, even the curtains have stopped twitching."

Death and darkness no longer lingered in the air; light now engulfed each nook and cranny of Oakley Place. Normality was resuming, and all the years were gathering and unfolding into a newness of expanding reality.

All five of them sat just watching the passing cars, the children on the village green happily playing and the folks of Oakley Place continuing about their ordinary lives.

Barney said, "Do you think they know what has happened? They all seem to be oblivious to the changes that have occurred in Oakley Place don't they? It feels kind of bizarre that no one will ever know, besides us, who are the only ones who truly know what has happened. I bet most of the villagers here in Oakley Place will also have never heard of Frederick de Soames or the 'Twitchers'."

Looking around and at each other, they all tried to take in what changes had taken place in all their lives.

Jasper, had already been struggling trying to readjust to life now that he had retired, and stopped his commutes into the Big Smoke. This only added to the confusion he had been feeling. The transition had been difficult, and he was now starting to see life from a whole new perspective.

Mrs Stanton was also finding the changes difficult; she did not fully comprehend that this had altered much more than she could see. Her age was clouding her view of life as it was now.

Both Jasper and Mrs Stanton, had loved and lived in Oakley Place for so long that neither now, had any idea how love would carry them both forward in their fading years.

They also knew that there would no longer be the need for either to carry on, for their lives were drawing in. They had both witnessed so much over the centuries. After all, they had both played out their many past lives through countless periods of history, and escaped from the ravages of various wars, to the dalliances of the 60s and 70s. Both sat blissfully reminiscing about their lifetimes together, and were held in deep conversation about the amazing and crazy things they had done, and indeed seen together during their travels across the canvas of history. Their journeys had taken them on many a voyage of discovery, which had at times carried them beyond mere immortality.

For as 'Wise Ones' their Divine duty and mission was to bring light, to find and protect the 'Illuminated Seekers', and reawaken love in the hearts of all mankind. Throughout the centuries they had met so many 'Illuminated Seekers', each one carrying a new clue and new answers, and each time their mission to regain equilibrium across time had evaporated.

This time though, Barney had been unaware of his role and his journey had been more a mistake than pre-planned destiny. Barney had brought them through the journey so far and it had been as a result of his actions that everything had changed, not only all their lives, but in the lives of many other people across all spaces and directions of time.

The veil of doubt had been torn asunder, and now the light of love could shine through and was able to rise up and out into an evolving World, that was slowly and effortlessly reawakening and reopening all hearts, bringing everything back to 'LOVE' and ' TRUTH'!

# Chapter Thirty-Two
# Back to the Beginning

Oakley Place was peaceful now that Frederick de Soames had spun off his mortal coil. Death had not come too soon to him, for he was death himself. Centuries of torture in Oakley Place had been a brutal payback for being put into the ground before his years had had a chance to roll in. Through the passage of time his essence had merged with the earth, and like the roots of a mighty oak, it had spread across the whole village. It travelled through deep veins within the earth – leaching out like a poison, which filtered into the very rivers, streams and air. It polluted the lifeblood of Oakley Place.

Barney was chatting on the village green, saying his final farewells to Ms Pemberton, Alice, Harold and Reginald.  It was time for him to move on to start a new life. Barney was moving to pastures new – to begin his journey once more.

He would not be leaving 'Oakley Place' alone; he would be accompanied on his journey by Jasper and Mrs Stanton.

The elderly couple had both grown frailer in recent days. They were also now ready to put the past behind them. Age had eroded both Jasper and Mrs Stanton, and during recent weeks they had also received visits from Jasper's son and daughter.

Barney overheard Jasper's son and daughter chatting, "I think we need to have dad living with us now; it looks like he really needs our support and help. Do you think dad and Mrs Stanton's carer, Barney, will want to carry on looking after dad and Mrs Stanton? After all, he seems quite good at his job and he's keen. It looks like he has been doing a reasonable job. Should we ask him if he'd mind, Marilyn? They could all come and either live at your place or at mine; we've both got bucketloads of space. You never know, he may say yes. After all, the old woman will be coming as well, considering she's supposedly shacked up with dad."

Barney didn't want to interfere.

He didn't think Jasper would want to leave and he definitely knew that Jasper would not leave without his beloved Mrs Stanton. It was quite sweet really, especially as they were both in the twilight of their years.

Later that day Jasper's son and daughter cornered Barney, and invited him to join them both in the garden away from Jasper and Mrs Stanton's ears.

"Excuse me, young man, could we possibly have a quick chat about our dad?" said Mr Swift, Jasper's son.

Barney didn't like the tone of the question.

"Mr Swift, what is it you want to know? If you think I'm sponging off your dad or Mrs Stanton – I'm not! It was your dad's idea for me to live here. I'm happy to move out if that's what you and your sister, Mrs Dart, want me to do? I completely understand it is a tad odd a young adult living with two old folk, who are not even related. When do you want me to go? Shall I start packing now? Would you mind if I just go and say goodbye to Jasper and Mrs Stanton? After all, they've both been better than any real parent really."

Jasper's son, Alex Swift, and daughter, Marilyn Dart, looked at Barney confused. Shuffling in the metal garden chair Alex said, "My sister Marilyn and I cannot thank you enough for all you've done for our dad – you've obviously made a big difference. It's been a good while since we have had a chance to come back to visit – what with one thing and another and well, you know how it is, before you know it life has whizzed by just like that."

There was an uncomfortable lapse in the conversation as Mrs Stanton poked her head out of the door, to see what was going on. Alex continued once she had stopped being nosy and had returned back into the kitchen.

Alex continued, "Barney, do you get the chance to see your folks much?"

Smiling a wry smile, Barney nodded, but was not prepared to give voice to his thoughts.

"Alex, your dad and Mrs Stanton, are great to look after – I've been here caring for them both for quite a while. We've had good days and bad days. We always take the rough with the smooth here – if you know what I mean?"

Barney nudged Alex, and gave him a cheeky wink.

Marilyn had now popped back out to join them both in the garden, as she had been distracted by a phone call from one of her business partners. Alex looked at his sister and spoke to her about his conversation with Barney. He said, "Barney was just saying he's been looking after dad and Mrs Stanton for ages. Marilyn, what do you think about Barney coming back with us to carry on looking after dad and Mrs Stanton? It would certainly reduce care costs and prevent us putting them both in a private care home – you know how costly those places can be, don't you? What do you think?"

Marilyn was too engrossed in firing off emails. She looked up and said, "Yes, absolutely, Alex, love, whatever you say."

Alex smiled at Barney, "The high and mighty – that is my dear sister, has spoken. So I think we can safely say, yes! You're coming to live with us all and Mrs Stanton and dad. We'll make sure you're suitably recompensed. How does that sound to you, Barney? You see, neither my sister nor I will have the time, to be brutally honest, Barney, and you've been doing such a great job and have time to look after them both to the high level they both deserve."

Barney said, "Yes, but of course – just let me know what's needed."

Alex and Marilyn got up from the garden chairs, and went back into the house to speak to Mrs Stanton and their dad.

Marilyn was a glamorous woman and they both looked as if they were minted. Both of them with more money, than Barney could have ever imagined. The total opposite of him, Mrs Stanton and Jasper; they were nothing like them at all. Jasper, Mrs Stanton and Barney were so down to earth in their ways, and Barney was unsure how it would work with their high-and-mighty ways. But he had no option, and it was time now to start anew. This may have been his only golden opportunity to live the life he knew he deserved, and had wanted for so long.

Mrs Stanton scurried out of the kitchen. Barney almost collided with her, as she went back into the kitchen where she was busily preparing one of her legendary cream teas for them all.

Barney bobbed his head around the door of the living room and said, "Alex and Marilyn, can you both just give me half an hour to think, so that I can be sure I'm going to be doing the right thing? I'll be back soon. Although I'm certain it will be a definite — Yes!"

Leaving the living room, Barney left Jasper's house. He wanted to take some air and have a stroll around Oakley Place one last time.

Passing thoughts drifted in and out of his head. Barney was keeping a deep secret, and there was no other choice but to leave with Jasper and Mrs Stanton. His hand plunged into his jacket pocket. In relief he sighed, feeling the coldness of the talisman. Although Frederick de Soames and the memory of him were no more, Barney sensed that there may be more ahead of them. Secrets would always live between Barney, Jasper, Mrs Stanton,

Alice and Ms Pemberton.

Decision made, the day had finally arrived. The removal van was being packed and Jasper and Mrs Stanton seemed rejuvenated and excited about their next adventure.

Who knew where it may lead, and what may lie ahead of them all?

For how did anyone know what was real?

Are we not just thoughts created by time and space?

# Chapter Thirty-Three
# Unknown Road

The future was the light at the end of the tunnel, of what had been a long and winding, if not turbulent road, for Barney. His life had twisted and turned, like a rollercoaster plummeting, through highs and lows. Sometimes taking him to the brink of insanity. Barney sat alone in the centre of the village green in Oakley Place. The birds sang in the trees above his head, without a care.

The removal van was just about to pull off, and had started slowly moving away from what had been Jasper and Mrs Stanton's front door. Mrs Stanton and Jasper had gone with Jasper's son Alex, to their new life far from what they had always known to the love of their family.

Ms Pemberton, Alice, Reginald and Harold all as dust— no longer even a whisper on the breeze.

All had also left Oakley Place behind them, like a fading memory.

Lost in his own mind, Barney sat, thoughts bombarding his brain like exploding shells of missiles. Thudding against his silent soul.

*' I wish I could just be on my own without anyone watching me, they're always just there watching me,'* he thought. *'There, can you see them? Although the curtains have stopped twitching they're still there. Barney, come on, wake up, wake up, stop dreaming.'*

Tiredness. Sleep-deprived. Barney now sat silent looking out through searching eyes.

*' Love,'* he thought, *'was that the answer? Could he be loved? Could he find love? Why hadn't my parents loved me? What did I do that was so wrong? Was I so bad? Why did I end up here? What was all this about? When can I go back to the beginning please and start over again?'*

Barney's head was in his hands; tears sliding down his pale complexion. Each teardrop transparent: unique and delicate. His mind: fractured and fragile. Pain leaching: out through his skin.

A car waited across from the village green, a person stepped from the car and stood motionless, watching Barney, just watching.

Children stopped as if moving slowly.

Life.

Everything around Barney swirled around him, as if a tornado had opened up above his head and all was being drawn into its core.

The colours and hues of life were fading into the whiteness of the day. Blending and merging, within each grain of Barney's life. The patterns of his existence: now shifting in his immersive youthful mind. Barney wondered if death would be so sublime.

Hidden within his grasp was a bottle, the label ripped on the side rendering it unreadable. Nursing the bottle, Barney sat thinking if he should. Alone now, the road ahead, though brighter, seemed endless and full of a minefield of hidden traps, waiting and eager to snap at their young prey. Barney looked once more at the bottle of pills. How easy it would be: one second and it could all be over, so swift; the nightmare to be etched no more within his soul.

He unscrewed the lid of the bottle, emptying the contents into his sweaty palm. There were twelve shiny little plastic-looking capsules. He wasn't even sure what they were for; they had just been left on the set of drawers in his old bedroom. Thinking deeply he took his hand near his mouth. Life balanced in the ebb and flow as if in one giant gulp it would all be over.

He did not for one second think, nor had he thought, about the agony of death to those he would leave behind.

Jasper and Mrs Stanton may not have many years ahead of them, but life was always full of surprises.

Tears stained his face. He stopped. His hand shaking, as he tossed the pill bottle to the ground, and his other hand loaded with pills shot forward, jettisoning the pills in front of him. It was as if someone or something had stopped him just in the nick of time. His fears receded.

Was this the result of all that had reeled him in throughout his life?

Suicide was not the answer, nor could it ever be.

*'At least I now have options, don't I? Maybe a new life with Jasper and Mrs Stanton. I'm just so afraid, that this entire nightmare I've lived through and grown up with is going to reopen somewhere down the line like a rotten fly-blown can of worms. Don't I, Barney, deserve to get my dreams in life? You know, to be loved just for me instead of what folks expect. I thought about my parents, Harriett and Jeremy, and wondered when they'd be rearing their ugly heads in my life again, or even if they would ever show up like bad pennies looking for me again? As far as I was concerned never would have been soon enough. I would ever see Ms Pemberton, Alice,*

Reginald and Harold ever again. *What had happened to John Yarrow, Penny and Silvia?'*

Barney wondered where they had gone and what had happened to them all.

So many unanswered questions pounded in his head.

The person, who had been watching Barney, stood across on the other side of the village green, admiring their shiny bright red high gloss sports car – just watching and waiting.

*'My mobile phone buzzed in my pocket. I didn't answer it; I needed to get my head space clear. I got up and stood on the village green, looking around me to check if anyone was watching. All was still, no signs of twitching curtains. The only watcher was the person standing next to the sports car. Well, it was now maybe the right time to leave Oakley Place, to take a leap of faith into the big open space. To look with wide-open eyes out into the distance of the unknown road materialising before me. I looked at my mobile phone to see who had tried to contact me. It was a missed text from Jasper all jumbled by predictive text. It seemed he just wanted to know where I was and if I'd be with them all soon. I just sent a quick message back saying I'd be there soon. I walked towards the person standing next to the bright red Ferrari and could now see that it was Jasper's daughter, Marilyn Dart. She looked glamorous in her Armani designer suit and smelt of Chanel. The perfume reminded me*

*of my mum.'*

Marilyn peered over her Gucci sunglasses, "Hi Barney, shall we go? I saw you sitting on the village green there, but I didn't want to disturb or interrupt you. It looked as if you were putting some ghosts to rest. I always think that's a good thing to do before moving on in life. Less chance they can come back to haunt you later on, isn't that right, Barney?"

Marilyn Dart smiled and opened the car door carefully.

"Marilyn, thank you for everything – let's just go. Jasper can't wait for us to get there to them."

Marilyn laughed, "Come on then, Barney. We mustn't keep dad and everyone waiting, must we?"

Marilyn Dart and Barney Lumsden drove off. Oakley Place left in the dust of their car wheels.

Oakley Place was now a fading distant memory.

Barney took one last look from the passenger seat window. The road winding out before them, wide and long.

Ahead of Barney, who knows what may lie in front of his growing years, rolling out and opening up as a fragrant rose unfolding its petals and reaching the light to find love and life's rich tapestry in which all things change and grow.

He wondered if there would be something waiting and watching.

He smiled to himself.

Let's just wait and see…

*'Life is just full of infinite possibilities, but LOVE always holds the key!'*

A little bit more about Barney, this book and me
the author...

# Acknowledgement

It is with thanks and gratitude to my wonderful husband Max and our amazing daughter Phoebe, for your never-ending love and support while I've been busy writing this book over the years.

Special thanks to my parents, who brought me into the world and taught me to never give up and to always believe in love!

Special thanks and gratitude to the lovely editor, Anna Paterson, who without her fantastic skill, endless support and encouragement the book would not have been finished and here.

Special thanks also to Editor, Richard Sheehan, for helping me to find Anna Paterson.

I would also like to give thanks to my extended family and friends who have plied me with tea, cake and bucketloads of support: Naomi, Sam, Nikki, Katie and Eve to name just a few of my friends who have been on hand with a cuppa and a smile!

Special acknowledgements to: Mike Dooley, a truly enlightened person and author of '*Infinite Possibilities: The Art of Living Your Dreams*', '*An Adventurer's Guide to the Jungles of Time and Space: Passport and Journal*' and '*Notes from the Universe:*

*New Perspectives from an Old Friend* '; Rhonda Byrne: creator of '*The Secret* ';

Poet, Deborah M. Hodgetts, for the poem titled: '*I Love You!* ' Which is taken from Deborah M. Hodgetts Poetry Collection publication entitled '*A Universe of Love* ';

The Parish Council and villagers of the real 'Oakley' in Bedfordshire and Buckinghamshire borders;

Steven Porter, author and excellent authority on all and everything to do with the plague.

A homeless, street artist friend and advisor on all things to do with living on the street, Elgan (Lee) Wilde, who is so wise, kind and compassionate – thank you!

And most importantly I would like to thank you all for reading this book and sticking with myself, Barney and his friends along the journey.

Hope to see you all in another place and time…

The Universe is full of Infinite Possibilities — just believe!

# ABOUT THE AUTHOR

**This is me...**

I am Deborah M. Hodgetts: a Published Poet in the UK and USA, Author of Young Adult novels, News Columnist, Freelance writer, Artist, Photographer, Screenwriter and Creative mind.

I live in a leafy village in the glorious countryside of Buckinghamshire, surrounded by beautiful nature, which always provides ample inspiration.

To find out more about me, and my writing you can usually find me in the following places: Twitter, Facebook, and Linked In.

Please pop by to my blog:

'The Beautiful Music of Words' or visit my website to see news on new publications, competitions and promotions.

I look forward to seeing you soon...

Deborah x

For further information about any of the issue's raised in this book please speak, support and connect with the following organisations and charities.

Your help would be greatly appreciated - thank you!

NSPCC

Shelter

Streetwise

Childline

Mind

May Day Trust

Big Issue

Salvation Army

Centrepoint

Crisis

Emmaus UK

Please look out for my E-book on homelessness titled

'The Only Home I Know' due to be released in late 2017.

A percentage of royalties from sales of ' The Curtain Twitchers of Oakley Place' and ' The Only Home I Know' will be donated to homeless charities and organisations across the UK/World.

## Other titles by Deborah Hodgetts:

**'A Universe of Love'**

Published by Blurb in 2017

ISBN: 978-1-36-628447-1

**'Applause Now Please!' -** E-book published by

Cut-a-long Story 2015

**Anthologies:**

**'Stray Branch - Autumn/ Fall 2016'**

ISBN: 978-1-5377-46739

**'Cover to Cover'-** Published by Forward

Poetry Social in 2013  (Out of Print)

**'A Day In Time' -** Published by Forward

Poetry Social in 2013  (Out of Print)

**'One-Week Poetry Challenge' -** Published by Forward

Poetry Social 2013  (Out of Print)

www.ingramcontent.com/pod-product-compliance
Lightning Source LLC
Chambersburg PA
CBHW061559190726
48288CB00007B/2099